LIGHTS OUT

LIGHTS OUT

a true story of a man's descent into blindness

L. SUBRAMANI

EBURY PRESS

An imprint of Penguin Random House

EBURY PRESS

USA | Canada | UK | Ireland | Australia
New Zealand | India | South Africa | China | Singapore

Ebury Press is part of the Penguin Random House group of companies whose addresses can be found at global.penguinrandomhouse.com

Published by Penguin Random House India Pvt. Ltd
4th Floor, Capital Tower 1, MG Road,
Gurugram 122 002, Haryana, India

Penguin Random House India

First published by Random House India 2014

Illustrations by Anukriti Sharma

10 9 8 7 6 5 4 3 2

ISBN 9788184003512

Typeset in Sabon by R. Ajith Kumar

Printed at Repro India Limited

www.penguin.co.in

FSC www.fsc.org MIX Paper from responsible sources FSC® C047271

This is a legitimate digitally printed version of the book and therefore might not have certain extra finishing on the cover.

To my spiritual gurus who have helped me sail over several storms and strengthened me with their inspirational words and deeds.

To the parents of millions of patients with Retintitis Pigmentosa who go through the heart-wrenching experience of watching their children go blind, like my own parents: Mrs Vijayalakshmi and Lakshmi Narayanan.

To all my mates at the English Literature course who will always remain my loving friends.

To all the teachers and priests at Loyola College, Chennai. The institution is an intellectual powerhouse and spiritual aboard for all its students.

Let us hope that this tale of darkness provides solace to many who fight a losing battle with blindness.

Contents

Author's Note ix

1. A Trip to the Doctor 1
2. The Changed World 15
3. Shadows of an Unknown Sin 25
4. Chasing Empty Hopes 35
5. A Rude Awakening 47
6. The Unseen Shadow 63
7. A Fugitive from Fear 81
8. The Setback and a Chance 93
9. The Illusion of Normalcy 103
10. The Persisting Blur 115
11. A Timeless Vista 127
12. The Descent Begins 137

Acknowledgements 157
A Note on the Author 161

Author's Note

'That which does not kill us makes us stronger'
—Friedrich Nietzsche

The idea of writing a book about my condition occurred while I was working with a network of fellow patients. As a part of an activity at the voluntary group, we took calls of people affected with retinal disorders and answered their queries on rehabilitation, training, and, most importantly, cure. While we found it easy to direct the patients to NGOs that offered services like mobility, computer training, and educational skills development, answering queries about rehabilitation and cure always made us uneasy. The fact is there is no cure for most of the retinal disorders that make a person progressively blind over a period of time. Sadly, most people think that finding a cure alone can solve their problems.

As fellow patients, our primary job is to let people know that they, like most of us in the network, can lead a perfectly normal life without letting their diminishing vision affect their confidence and self-esteem. But a major part of the problem is their way of living and society that puts them in the confines of limitations. Their lifestyle does not let them get out of their comfort zones or challenge themselves. Most people are unaware that technology can solve most of the problems faced by patients experiencing progressive vision loss. Unfortunately, there is lack of awareness and reassurance that there is life after blindness and that, in fact, there is a way for patients to fashion themselves as inspiring role models rather than become victims of an incurable condition. While working with the network, I realized that awareness is the only way to change the situation and so I wanted to solve it in the only way I know: write. I wanted to write a book instead of an article because I wanted to create a platform to speak about the disorder that has specifically affected me and a million others in India.

I also realized in the process that retinal disorders do not just affect a small segment of the population.

From a global perspective it might sound alarming, but India has millions of patients suffering from retinal disorders. In fact the condition I suffer from is just one of the many categories of retinal disorders. Imagine the impact of dealing with so many patients without any awareness about the condition. There is a high possibility that a person affected by such a problem could go blind either slowly, over several years or in a matter of months. In India, we don't really know how to accommodate children with retinal disorders in our schools and what to do if someone were afflicted with it. It is alright to boast about our human capital and demographic dividend, but we can only let that advantage slip if we are not prepared to handle a large number of people with genetically pre-disposed conditions (affecting many organs including the retina), as a result of intra-family marriages and consanguinity (blood relationship), which is so common in our country.

This book is meant to describe the physical, mental, and psychological condition of a person experiencing progressive blindness and the way it affects his family. Along with these issues, the book is about having strength in the face of adversity. It tells you that dreams can survive even in potentially nightmarish situations and love is the only way to heal emotional wounds. It talks not only about a specific retinal disorder, but also how vital it is to help a person who cannot lead a normal life or pursue his education or job because of certain significant limitations. My purpose of writing this book will be served if it conveys to the reader that every person with vision disorder is essentially facing similar problems like others. For a disabled person, the possibility of living a normal life is not something that should be looked at in isolation. In fact, his success depends a great deal on how accommodative the society is and how his environment aids in the pursuit of his dreams.

Also, I have utmost regard for alternative medicinal system, but in the context of an incurable condition, which I am describing in the book, there is no specific scientific validation to back up claims that they can provide a cure. So unless science gives us an indication that alternative therapies do make a difference, it is not proper to delude patients into believing that they can actually work. Needless to mention, I think it is a drain on the precious little resources that patients and families have for their survival. Also, as a pious man myself, the attempt to describe rituals is to highlight that while they can be a great source of inner strength that can help reconcile with any situation, it is inappropriate to take them as a means to finding a cure. Similarly spiritual quests must lead us to true teachers and gurus and not those who promise non-existent cures for the sake of money.

In this book, I have changed some of the names of people close to me to protect their identity and largely to keep the focus on the overall story. Chronological orders of certain events have been changed to make the narrative smoother, but the time period and the incidents described are all real.

L. Subramani

ONE

A Trip to the Doctor

Madras on an August morning—there is nothing quite so energetic. And there is no city quite so resistant to that inhumanity typical of urban life. It is August 1988. I have turned 15 just a few weeks ago.

I am now heading to my new school.

The wooden door of my house lets out a mild squeak as I open it to stare at the busy street lit up by the bright sun. I step out and walk the length of just one house, before turning left into Wall Tax Road that will take me to the legendary Madras Central Station. Here, the road from Pallavan House meets with Poonamallee High Road, forming a perfect perpendicular. A torrent of traffic gushes in from all directions, churning and swirling like a whirlpool. Thank God, I do not need to use the zebra crossing here since my bus stop is close to the underground walkway. I just follow the pavement above Cooum river, a handkerchief clamped over my nose, of course, and descend the wide steps of the underground walkway to emerge on the other side of the road.

Three months ago, I cleared my SSLC. I would like to add 'with flying colours' but no, my 70 percent was a reinforcement of my status as a barely above average student. Having no appetite for science or engineering, I am happy to take up the commerce stream in my higher secondary. My new school is just a bus ride away and I am still warming up to the new campus.

I'm one of the three or four boys in my class who wear spectacles, and all of us are nicknamed 'Four Eyes'. While the other bespectacled boys have rid themselves of their 'nerd' image by playing cricket or football, I have no such redemption. I stay away from the sporting arena, and feel content to stick to the confines of my classroom.

That's why I am surprised when Geeth, my classmate, walks up to me to ask if I can be a defender in the football game that evening. Geeth is assembling a group to play against Johnson and his boys, also from my class.

'Why don't you play with ten? It's just an informal practice match.'

'That's right, but we need to strategize and that means all positions have to be filled. Why don't you help us out?'

I could have, if for no other reason than to put an end to the taunts of 'Four Eyes', but I have an appointment with my ophthalmologist scheduled this evening, and I know I can't miss it for the world.

Geeth is unhappy, but I'm sure he will eventually understand. I watch his tall, lanky frame disappear amid a sea of white shirts and khaki trousers. From the back, you can't tell that he wears glasses—not even a bit of the frame is visible. Maybe it looks like that for me too, I hope.

I've discovered now that these guys are nice and friendly, but I am still not completely over the embarrassment they had caused me at the first physical education class. It's hard to forget the day when we squirmed under the harsh sun without refuge. The playground was broad, the canopy of trees lining the compound wall looking far and distant as an oasis in a desert. A few of us used our handkerchiefs to wipe our sweaty foreheads while our physical education teacher, Mr Sami, helped separate us into six different groups. Some boys were welcomed into their group with a pat on their back, while the others were picked more randomly, less enthusiastically. Finally, I was the only one left standing, alone, not chosen, with absolutely no one wanting me in their team.

It didn't take long to realize why. Besides the spectacles, I didn't fit in the 'sporty' image and was taking time to warm up to my new environment. I may be a recluse who often kept his face buried behind books, but I was still a boy who wanted to be a part of the group; who wanted to belong. That morning though, I came to the shocking realization that the shy hesitation was being met with a cold indifference I had never experienced before. My spectacles, more than my attitude, was creating a fence which no one wanted to breach. The world, after all, can't be equal or even friendly for everyone!

This fence started to envelope me from the age of 5, when I fixed the thick black spectacles frame over my nose for the first time with considerable struggle. The idea that the glasses I wore was more valuable than the urge to run around with other boys or kick a ball was drilled into me from then on. I have grown up thinking that wearing glasses precluded my doing the most natural of things. A covey of over-protective elders did little to change this impression. I remember the humiliation of having to play cricket with a football, and I still had trouble seeing the ball because my aunt removed my glasses for safekeeping.

'Don't run around and break your glasses!' elders in my family would scream. 'Don't walk alone at night!'; 'Don't chase after your brother!' 'Don'ts is all I have heard since childhood. There's little wonder that fear has become a part of me like the spectacles I have grown up hating.

That afternoon, I leave school earlier than usual. Stepping out of the corridor, I turn around to see the vast playground behind the main building where Geeth, Johnson, and their respective teams swarm around the football, eager for the first dribble. I mumble 'good luck' to them as I hurry out of the gate.

The appointment with Dr Rakesh is a joyful yearly ritual, almost like my birthday. The reason? It usually results in a new pair of glasses. With each passing year, I am more determined to convert these glasses, my object of weakness and impairment, into a fashion statement—something that might make me look intellectual, even attractive. The idea brings a smile to my face and I notice a man in the aisle of our almost-empty bus, giving me a perplexed look. I quickly adjust my demeanor with a faint nod and a sweet smile before moving further down the aisle.

The sun has almost dipped below the western horizon, as I enter the familiar gates of Dr Rakesh's clinic. From a distance, the place looks like any other posh residence on this side of the city—compound walls painted greyish white and a small portico lined with decorative pots containing slender plants. The waiting area with a row of chairs arranged along the creamy white walls clearly indicates that this indeed is a clinic. Patients, occupying most of them, lean their heads on the small headboard fixed above the chairs to save the walls from oily imprints. Tears are rolling down their cheeks, but they make no effort to open their eyes. With enough experience of subjecting myself to dilation, I know what it feels like when the liquid is poured into the eyes—the burning sensation—as if acid has touched its sensitive surface.

I enter the semi-lit consultation chamber and stretch on the reclining chair. I bite my lip and with little desperation, try to stop the tears from rolling down when the scorching beam of light from the ophthalmoscope pierce my pupils. The examination is as painful as half an hour of dilation that preceds it. Even as the probing of my eyes' interiors continue, I notice Dr Rakesh lingering over his ophthalmoscope a tad longer than usual. His smiling face goes taut with anxiety as he continues the examination. He doesn't exactly say that something is wrong with my eyes, but he looks concerned. He asks us to come back the next day. This is not unusual, given that filling out the prescription form usually takes a day, but this time the doctor has asked us to fix an appointment. 'I have a few more tests to do on his eyes,' Dr Rakesh tells mother in an even voice. She usually escorts me to these eye tests.

I feel impatient. The glasses—that's all I want right now. I've already checked out a beige, slim frame for myself, which I think would look really nice with photo-chromatic lenses that turn a sophisticated brown in the sun.

The next afternoon, my mother and I are back at the doctor's. My eyes are still reeling from the previous day's dilation, and the bright afternoon sun doesn't help. I don't think about the tests that the doctor wants to run. Instead, I focus on the beige spectacles that I have set my mind on. I can't wait to get this over with.

'We don't need a dilation today,' Dr Rakesh dismisses the suggestion of his clinical assistant, and watches me as I sigh in relief. 'Why don't you lie down on the couch?' he tells me. 'I need to give your eyes a good check.' He gestures towards the couch that almost fills the far end of the room. This is definitely odd—I've been coming here for nearly three years, and not once have I been directed to the couch.

The doctor stares down at me with a bright instrument strapped to his forehead. He asks me to keep my eyes open, but the beam of light hitting my eyes hurt and pierces my pupils with the force of a bullet. I gasp. The examination is an unending torture that makes dilation seem like a pin-prick. The pain is continuous, unrelenting, and it almost pushes me to the threshold of tolerance. Just as my head starts to shake in pain and tremendous discomfort, a sharp snap of a switch puts out the source of my agony. A minute of blissful darkness follows, and I take a series of deep breaths to relax my stiff muscles and joints. I find it difficult to get up for a few more minutes, lying on the couch, unable to shrug off the paralysing effect of the examination.

Dr Rakesh usually smiles when he speaks to me. He asks questions about a thousand trivial things just to divert my mind from the impending pain or the intensity of the test. Why didn't he try any of these today, I wonder? Even now, as he is looking down at me, there's no trace of a smile on his face.

'Do you mind stepping outside for a while?' I've never heard him sound so plain and cold.

'You mean…outside this room?'

'Yes. I'd like to have a word with your mother alone.'

The initial confusion gives way to shock and anger. What does this doctor think of me anyway? I'm 15, sport a moustache, and I am perfectly capable of being present in the room to listen to my own diagnosis. I have to blink many times before I can see the door to the waiting hall and pull its handle. The blast of light from the well-lit waiting room is enough to drive back the pain. Eyes firmly shut, I breathe deeply once again to relax my stiffening joints and trembling hands. Thankfully, I don't spend too much time in finding the nearest chair.

It is almost five in the evening. The perfectly square waiting hall appears smaller, as a stream of patients walk in through the portico and mill around the reception desk to announce their arrival for an appointment. Before my thoughts drift in the direction of the eye problems that has brought so many patients to the clinic, I feel Dr Rakesh's hand pressing on my shoulder. I tilt my head up to listen to what he has to say. 'Just the usual tests my boy', or 'Nothing to worry about, or 'Here's your prescription, now go and get your new glasses,' might have been nicer to hear.

But instead he asks me, 'So, ready for school from tomorrow?'

There must be something more than that... I watch his face expectantly.

But the doctor merely pats my shoulder, mumbles a weak 'good luck', and walks back into his consultation room. I turn towards mother thinking that she has got a prescription for new glasses. It's already past five and we must hurry to the optical stores to buy my favourite frame and place the order today. However, one look at her face, and I freeze in cold terror.

She's crying. Tears stream down her cheeks. She's crying in the full view of strangers, I realize with shock, something I have never seen her do before. 'God, Ma! What happened? What did he tell you?' I ask, unable to control my horror.

I shake her shoulders, ignoring the several heads that have already turned in our direction. 'What's happened? What did he say?'

'He says... Oh god, what will I do?'

'Ma... Please. Tell me what happened!'

'He says you're going blind.'

'Blind? How? I can see now!'

'He says you have a condition that will gradually make you go blind,' she tells in a wheezy whisper, the shiny tears still rolling down her cheeks.

'What!'

She wipes her eyes with a handkerchief, draws a deep breath, and says, 'It's a condition called Retinitis Pigmentosa. It'll eventually make you blind.'

It is my turn to take a deep breath. 'Okay Ma, okay. Let's find out if there's a cure for this condition. We can still do something about it,' I say in a weak, unconvincing voice, and immediately receive the second blow.

'Cure? No... He says there's none.'

TWO

The Changed World

Darkness stares back at us from the recesses of our home as mother unlocks the main door and steps in. She walks along the corridor turning on the lights, but the silvery glow of the mercury vapour only reflects our gloomy faces. She sits heavily on the floor in the hall, not bothering to wipe away the tears on her pallid face.

By now, news of the diagnosis has reached Dad. Ma stopped by his office and filled him in. He followed us home and saw mother lying on the cold floor of the hall, sobbing uncontrollably. Sitting by her side, I can do nothing but watch her helplessly, working hard to control my own urge to throw myself on the floor next to her and cry my heart out because the world seems to have become a lot gloomier from the moment we left Dr Rakesh's clinic. What has happened to our happy home? Have we lost it forever to an inexplicable eye condition?

'You shouldn't be worrying like this,' Dad tells Ma, squatting beside her and nervously patting her back. The picture of my parents staying together at this time seems more worrying than comforting. Of course, it's natural for the head of the family to stand by his loved ones at the time of such crisis. But Dad is basically a nervous man who can't conceal his fears with a mask of courage. He has had shoulders to lean on all his life. Now he has a challenge on his hands: to support his sobbing wife and distraught son. Despite doing his best, the nervousness is evident from the half-hearted words and slumped shoulders which only adds to the agony.

My father was raised in a joint family setup. It is therefore characteristic of him to immediately inform his siblings of the diagnosis. On any other occasion, I would have held that against him, but now, considering Ma's condition and his own, that seems like the best thing. He accounces, 'Raman Anna says he'll drop by and check the diagnosis himself'. That might actually help, I think to myself. Uncle Raman, Dad's older brother and a doctor, might be able to tell something that will comfort them, even help them deal with this better. If this RP condition is really as bad as Dr

Rakesh has made it out to be, then Ma needs all the support she can get, and so does my father.

'This is just one doctor's diagnosis. You shouldn't be disheartened. Let's see what Anna has to say about it,' he tries again to console my mother. There's some conviction in his voice this time, and that seems to brighten mother's face a bit.

'Did Anna really say that? Did he say that something can be done about it?'

'Yes, yes, why don't you relax for a while and wait until he comes?'

My parents look devastated despite their frantic attempts to comfort each other. I watch them in that state and wonder if we are actually over-reacting. Probably we are. I can see the point in what Dad just said. There is certainly room for a second opinion and a thorough understanding which would help us find a way to handle this situation. To me, blindness or vision impairment is no different than coming across a three-eyed monster on our street corner. In short, I don't believe I'd go blind in five, fifty, or even hundred years, no matter what RP is supposed to do to my eyes. Then, what's the point of all this worry? I know I can't change my parents or the way they react. Even injured toes or bruised knees, which happened quite often in my childhood, made them extremely sad. Since I'm not a parent, I can only guess how they feel.

Except my uncle, I also know how my extended family would react to a news like this. It is typical of the Tamil Brahmins to squat before a silver jug and pour water on their palms with murmurs of prayers asking the God to cleanse our sins. They go on praying, until the Gods show up and grant their wish. Many of us believe that the answer to our problems can be found in prayer which is often considered an act of purification that removes sins. So all worldly remedies naturally take a back seat.

My parents' eyes sparkle when they see uncle Raman. Like a man on a mission, he pushes aside small talk and gets straight to the business at hand. He says, 'Show me the report.'

Uncle Raman is a tall and well-built man, with salt and pepper hair. Like many male members in my family, he pays little attention to sartorial splendours. You only need to take a look at his maroon shirt and olive trousers, neat but faded, to get a sense of our family's inherent indifference to dressing. A TB specialist with the government's Health Department, he has been raising my little brother Eshwar for the last two years.

There's tension, nervous anticipation, and

an agonizing mixture of hope and despair as three pairs of eyes watch uncle Raman read the report with intense concentration. We watch his face transform from shock and disbelief to grief as he comes to terms with the report. He removes a handkerchief from his trouser pocket and dabs his eyes, meaning to be discrete, not knowing how.

'It does sound serious,' he admits, massaging his forehead. 'But then, we should go for a second opinion. To see if the diagnosis is right.'

Unable to find any obvious flaws in Dr Rakesh's diagnosis, Dr Raman only insists on the need for a second opinion. It's quite possible that a different doctor could dismiss the idea of a degenerating genetic condition as improbable. He talks about impending family functions to change the subject, having noticed the glum faces and indifferent nods to his assessment. He perhaps realizes that his audience only wants to hear that the report is rubbish and the past few hours are nothing more than a bad dream.

Ma gets back into the kitchen to bring coffee and evening snacks for us; Dad has excused himself on the pretext of pending work. This is the chance I have been waiting for. I can finally speak to someone who knows about the reality of the situation that I find myself in. My uncle and I speak for some time about my new school, the new subjects and so on, but gradually I steer the conversation towards what I really want to speak about.

'This thing...this condition or whatever...is worrying them a bit too much, I think,' I say as I watch my father leaving. I notice my uncle suddenly going pale.

'Their fears aren't entirely unfounded. Now, I don't know how much your doctor has told you about this, but let me tell you that the genetic condition he has described has a very sound scientific basis,' he says, tapping the folded sheet of paper lying beside him. 'You may have learnt something about genetics in school. Genes form the foundational structure of the human body, just like bricks are laid in a particular manner to form the foundation of a building. Genes contain the basic programming of how various parts of our body will function. Retinitis Pigmentosa could happen when a particular series of bricks used in the foundation are defective.'

He looks at my face and continues, 'But the doctor could be wrong, you know. He has reached this conclusion only after studying your eyes. But there's every possibility that he could have misread the symptoms and come to a wrong conclusion. I'm not doubting his competency but he is human after all. And humans can make mistakes.'

He is breathing easier now because he is discussing the uncertainties, asking questions that could poke holes at Dr Rakesh's grim diagnosis, and giving me a strand or two of hope to hang on to. Of course, he's a man of science, can speak in expert jargon and emphasize on what needs to be done, but he is also my uncle. I notice how his eyes dart from right to left, never once meeting my own, making me feel uneasy. So, despite his words of assurance, uncle Raman knows. He knows that RP is real and is affecting my retina brick by brick! I break into a cold sweat.

'Is it true then?' My despairing question is almost inaudible, but my uncle has heard it. He does what any elder person would do. He walks up to me and gives me a comforting hug. If he noticed the wet patch on his shirt, he doesn't seem to bother about it.

'I just told you, right? Doctors are human. There's a force, a greater force above us that programmes our lives. We doctors are like fortune tellers; the only difference is that we're educated and can say confidently that we're qualified enough to make our predictions about health. But we can't play God, son. We can't do that.'

I don't tell him that there's another reason for my tears—this hug should have come from Dad. His hands should have patted my back and lifted my sagging spirits. But no. My father is used to getting comfort and not giving it. Not even to his children. How can he do that, when he's struggling to shake off his own uncertainties and fears? Dad is also not the reaching out kinds. He is timid, hesitant, and unsure of himself in emotionally challenging moments.

THREE

Shadows of an Unknown Sin

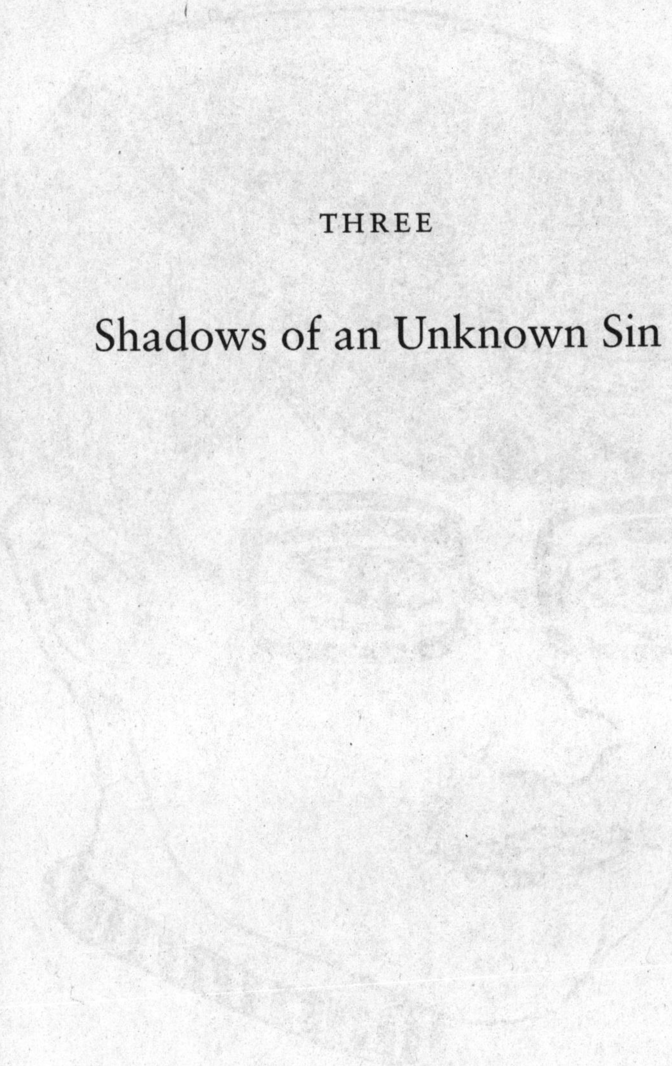

'You look different today!' Balu looks down at me, leaning against a large column at the edge of the corridor. In the new school, Balu is my closest friend. He is repeating the class and looks more like an adult than a student. His rebelliousness is what drew me to him when we first met some three weeks back. It was interesting to meet someone with a contrasting view of the world. Unlike me, Balu is a non-vegetarian, a loner, a non-believer, and a person who hates anything close to an establishment. He doesn't care about what others think of him.

'Do I really look different?' I ask Balu.

He nods, pointing at the sandalwood paste mark on my forehead, 'Haven't seen you wear that before. So, you too are a showman like them!' he says gesturing in the direction of the main gate behind me. I do not reply. It's hard to convince Balu that we can't always go against our beliefs, especially when our supposed normality is challenged. Convincing takes patience and time, and with someone like Balu, one can't be sure of the outcome. As if aware of what I am thinking, the bell rings, and both of us rush towards the classroom.

Balu catches up with me again in the evening. We join the throng of students leaving school, some on foot and others on bicycles. A sense of relief and happiness is clearly visible on our faces since we are going back home after the tedious hours at school.

'So, what's up?' he asks again, looking into my face.

In the frenzy that followed the diagnosis, I had forgotten all about the new school and the new subjects I would have to study. After weeks of fitful attendance, when I return to my class, I am reduced to the ignominy of staring at the blackboard with utter incomprehension. One teacher after another walks into the class, scribbles some random words on the board, spokes about things I had never heard before, and then walks out at the sound of the hourly bell, while I looks on, baffled and discouraged. I had always been an average student, but never before had things been this bad for me.

Not just in studies, but I seem to have fallen behind in almost everything that matters to young boys. For instance, during the lunch break, a few classmates were discussing the winners of the recently held Olympic events. A chill had run down my spine when I realized that I wasn't even aware that the games had begun. It felt as if I had been comatose for some weeks and had woken up only to realize that the world had moved on, without me.

'That guy,' I had stammered, trying to join in their conversation. 'You know, he won the maximum number of medals in Swimming. Mats Meyondi, isn't it?'

I intended to say Matt Biondi, but I blurted out something else. My friends' laughter felt like a slap on my face. I realized then that I shouldn't have spoken about things I didn't know for sure.

'Hey! Tell me, what's wrong?' asks Balu shaking my shoulders, and tears roll down my cheeks. At this moment, it feels right to pour out my heart and let Balu know of the diagnosis and its devastating impact. But I hold back, fearing that I might sound like a cry-baby before a friend and risk losing his respect and friendship.

'Can you do me a favour?' I ask.

'Oh sure. What do you want? Ask me anything,' Balu says anxiously.

'I won't be coming to school for a few more days.

Missing lessons will be a big problem for me. I've already missed out on a lot...'

'Oh, is that what is bothering you? You don't have to get upset about studies. I'll help you out with everything.'

'I really need your help, Balu. I won't be coming to school for some more time. It could be a week or even a month.'

'What are you going to do for so long?'

'Well...' I sigh, trying my best to come up with a believable excuse. 'There are a few prarthanas I need to do in the temples for my family's sake.'

'What! You mean to say that you are going to miss school so that you can offer prayers!' Balu smirks. 'Bribing God for a better future? Ha!'

'This is something my family wants me to do,' I say in a feeble voice, trying to regain my dignity.

I watch Balu taking deep breaths as he leaves. I could have easily confided in him the reality about the condition that scares me and my family. After all, he's a friend. But I'm weary of adding one more person to the list of skeptics, inclined to question the motives of the doctor rather than accepting his diagnosis. Moreover, I wouldn't like to become the object of sympathy among my peers.

Desperation spreads through me like a contagion

when I think about the long hours that my family and I have spent pondering about my condition. Commenting on its strangeness and symptoms, we have fallen silent again and again, realizing the impact it will have on our lives and our future.

The fact that the affliction could make me go completely blind fills us with dread. The very thought is enough to benumb my usually talkative family. Their frozen frame and terrified eyes give out the extent of their torment even as they try hard to go through with the daily tasks. Some of our relatives, who come home to console us, become inconsolable themselves as if it's they, not me, who is struggling with RP.

The more pious among them believe it's better to turn our desperation into undying devotion. They tell my mother that prostrating before god, begging for his mercy with tearful eyes, would help us find a way out. Recommendations of hymns and mantras to be chanted are promptly provided on scribbled sheets and handed over to me, along with the names of shrines and temples where I should offer my prayers and pleas for divine intervention.

I grew up with stories of divine intervention and the appearance of God before a steadfast devotee to grant his wishes. But getting rid of RP isn't a commonplace wish. Wavering between the hopelessness of the condition and the desperation to find a way out, I'm inclined to think that my prayers wouldn't be anything more than a frantic plea. Prostrating before a deity without a shred of love or devotion, but full of myself and my worries, isn't the idea of prayer that I learnt in those stories. Moreover, if God wants me to be the usual 15-year-old, I don't think I'll be here in the first place, and if he doesn't then I don't think he can be persuaded easily. I keep those thoughts to myself and prepare for some tough rituals to get rid of my sins if not the condition threatening my clear eyesight.

Belief in rituals is not such a danger when compared to the denial of the condition itself. Without obvious signs other than my short sight, some of my family members thought that the diagnosis is questionable. It could be a compelling argument, especially if you reject the idea of carrying an incurable eye disorder.

'How can a boy who was born with eyesight go blind suddenly? I think the doctor is out of his mind. Doctors these days fool their patients and then make money out of them,' claimed an uncle. Mother heard him out with an understanding smile, but maintained her silence. It was unlikely that she would take anything more than a measure of comfort from such absurd comments.

One solution, however, never fails to convince her—alternative therapy. Many claim that it is superior to allopathic medicines and its practitioners are not as exploitative as the Western doctors. Ma believes that alternative medicine has a cure for every ailment, even RP, and no matter how much I disagree with her or disapprove about such a therapy, when it comes to cooperating with Ma, I have no choice but to comply. After all, besides allaying my own fears about going blind, I need to ensure that Ma gets all her chances of trying to find me a cure.

FOUR

Chasing Empty Hopes

I abstained from going to school at Ma's urging. She believes it is possible to find a cure, only if we search for it. In fact, she has an idea of where to begin this search, thanks to suggestions that have poured in from family, friends, and strangers. They all scoffed at the idea of a sighted individual going blind due to an awful condition. 'What goes in between, comes in between', seems to be their opinion on RP, as they scratch out addresses of alternative therapists on a piece of paper or at the back of their visiting cards.

Ma also finds names of miracle workers, divine interventionists, astrologers and their type who all claimed to have knowledge of the past sins and the remedies to get rid of their effects. That Ma resorted to non-scientific methods is a measure of our desperation to hang on to the hope of a cure, however empty it might be.

I am still thinking about school and going back to classes when the autorickshaw I am sitting in, takes a bumpy ride along the narrow lanes of Triplicane. I am on my way to meet the latest godman on ma's list—a magician and a healer with clairvoyant powers. In spite of my disbelief and reservations about him, I am suddenly beginning to feel hopeful about the visit. Perhaps, if I quickly get through these consultations, I could soon go back to school as well.

'Just around the next corner,' my uncle tells us with a pleasant smile. He knows the tantrik personally and has got an evening appointment with 'great difficulty'. Even Ma—who has always been enthusiastic about meeting astrologers and gifted middlemen capable of summoning the natural forces—seems reluctant about meeting this one.

Our auto rickshaw stops in front of the small entrance of a house which seems no different from many along the crammy lane. We walk through a narrow, tunnel-like passage, and are directed to the farthest corner. This place looks more like a coal mine—dark, dusty, and suffocating. It occurs to me that if someone were to strangle us to death here, no other human being would have a chance of finding us. I wipe the thin layer of sweat from my forehead as I follow the two elders walking before me. Going ahead, we reach a stairway which is as dark and narrow as the passage.

As we turn left and climb another flight of stairs, light greets us. The reassuring orange glow of the evening sun floods into the passage from the open terrace above, and I begin to breathe easy.

At the other end of the open terrace, we notice a large platform. Placed atop is a picture of Goddess Durga, peering at us with menacing eyes. The wide cement vase at the centre of the room contains a heap of ash, smoke escaping out of the last few embers.

Our eyes eventually settle on the large human frame that sits on the ground before us. His forehead is smeared with three horizontal streaks of holy ash, and placed at its centre is a spot of vermilion, as big as a peach. I see a glint of gold and gems on his fingers as he raises his right hand to bless the prostrating figures.

He picks up the folded sheet of paper my mother offers to him and peers into it with the intensity of a grandmaster considering the pieces on a chessboard. His face turns grave when he looks at me and says, 'I feel sorry for this boy.' I try to read the intent behind his steady stare. 'This boy is the victim of a curse,' he declares. 'He has dragged with him the effects of a very bad curse from his previous birth. He's very impure! We have to cleanse him and make him worthy of the Goddess' blessings.'

Sweat begins to dampen my clothes and I notice that my mother isn't looking any better.

'Is there a way out? Swami, please tell us what we should do,' uncle asks the obvious question, at which the tantrik's face softens.

'Oh yes, yes, there's a way out, of course. There's always a way out, and that's exactly why the great Goddess has ordered us to help people like you,' the man says. He then closes his eyes to show us that he is overcome with divine energy by the mere mention of the Goddess' name. And then, he takes out a long sheet of paper.

'We should conduct a homa for him,' he says in an almost business-like voice. 'The homa has to be performed thrice. You will have to bring all the ingredients—flowers and garlands for the Goddess, a five-litre can of ghee, three pieces of silk cloth, along with five thousand and one rupees for conducting each of the homas—a simple donation for my services,' he announces.

He waits patiently as we do a quick mental calculation.

'Think of it this way... Your nephew will be completely cured when we cleanse him of the curse. He won't go blind. He'll do well in his studies, get a job, and be successful. Is it not even worth fifteen thousand rupees?'

Noticing Ma's discomfort, uncle smiles and says that he'll soon get back to the tantrik. With customary obeisance, we file out of the open terrace, descending the narrow and dark stairway. I'm wise enough to remain silent. Uncle knows the tantrik well, and I am aware that I must save my not-so-reverent comments for a later and more private time. As we take an autorickshaw for home, I promise myself that I'm done with all this. I tell Ma that if she wants to consult these middlemen again, she will have to do it on her own.

But barely days later, we're back on another visit to an alternative healer, and we're taking the train this time. 'We are going to visit a man, who is possessed by a divine spirit,' Ma informs me. It is late evening, and the sun's light has faded to a darkish grey. We soon reach one of those suburbs that always seem to fall silent when it gets dark. We move through the labyrinth of empty pathways and dense trees, and head towards the house at the corner of the street, the only one that is lit up so brightly.

As we enter the spacious hall, the Devi Upasaka looks up to meet our eyes. Unlike the tantrik his stare is milder and filled with kindness. I think, he even looks more credible. But before I can grow comfortable in his presence, he falls down on the floor suddenly, begins to twitch and roll around and crawl towards me. His eyes go blank, his mouth opens, and his right hand twists and makes slithering motion like a snake. His palm is cupped in the shape of a hood. His wife enquires if he is trying to show that 'the boy', that is me, 'has Naga Dosha.' His head bobs up and down in agreement. I notice the calm demeanor of his wife and wonder if she is used to the presence of a spirit in her husband's body. I'm grateful for her intervention because I don't know how to respond to the Upasaka's reptilian imitation. Then he goes limp and lies unconscious for a few minutes before rising from the ground and resuming his squatting position.

'Your son is carrying an impurity within him because he has offended or hurt a snake in some way. You must take him on a pilgrimage to Nattarasankotai, a shrine located near Madurai. Also offer a pair of silver eyes to the Goddess. This will cleanse him of his Naga Doshas.'

So again it seems that I am a product of impurity,

born with imperfection imperfections. I feel I am nothing more than a constant reminder to people around me of sin and its inevitable effects. All that people want to do, I realize, is somehow banish the idea of blindness from my life, even if it means reconstructing the positions of a few planets and correcting the cosmic mistake that has left me with the eye condition. But while they are at it, will they also do something about the defective gene that I carry, which is the real cause of my troubles?

My family's desperate search for a cure, of course, doesn't end at the parlours of godmen and astrologers. We next take a ride across the town to go to a small building in a rundown neighbourhood of Madras. We would have missed the building had it not been for the blue-green wooden doors displaying the door number prominently. We find a plaque fixed on one of the doors with 'therapist' written on it.

It opens into a small veranda with a bench on one side. To me, it seems more like a visitors' lounge. Photographs depicting mystical men flying, swimming, crawling, and displaying superhuman abilities cover the walls. Superheroes for sure, but I am not sure whether the cure for RP resides in their magical fingers.

The pungent odour of herbs and powders soon floats into the room, and I sneeze a few times. I try distracting myself by flipping through some magazines, stacked in the corner of the room, but escaping the stink seems next to impossible. I hold a handkerchief close to my running nose and peep inside the consultation room. I see the doctor engrossed in an animated conversation with some visitors. Ma, seated next to me, looks tired and sleepy.

'What's the problem with you?' a tall, thin man wearing a clean white khadi jibba asks my mother as he ushers us into the cramped cabin.

'I'm fine. This is about my son. He has a problem with his eyes,' she replies.

For the next ten minutes, she explains to the therapist every detail she has learnt from Dr Rakesh.

'I can work on this. This should be curable,' the therapist assures us with a warm smile.

While there is no direct reference to RP in the system of what he practices, he assures us that he's familiar with my symptoms. That does the trick and Ma, in no time, signs up for the therapy, which only means that I'll have to consume a bagful of obnoxious medicines.

The transport, medical expenses, and fees that

we have had to pay to the different godmen has cost us a heavy chunk of our monthly savings. Our family business has many partners, and those who manage it with my father, prefer grandpa's frugality when it comes to taking out money for personal expenses. But as always, Ma juggles with whatever money she has.

For want of a better place, mother converts a section of my bookshelf into a medicine cabinet. Beside the stack of textbooks and notebooks, she lines up an impressive stock of tablets in multiple colours. There are also a number of tonics and powders standing tall like dikes along a river bed. Every day, I force myself to swallow them, if not for my own comfort, at least for mother's sake. Our effort to stop RP in its tracks may not be scientific, but the fact that we're doing something about it is a great comfort. Of course, we need the illusion of a cure to resist the thought of blindness and to keep the idea of loos of vision at bay. And it seems to be working, at least in reinforcing our belief, however false it may be.

FIVE

A Rude Awakening

I jump down from the bus and rush towards the zebra crossing. I want to reach the other side before the 'WALK' sign goes off. Only half an hour ago, the crossing would have been flooded with children in white and khaki uniforms heading towards the school, but now there are only adults, mostly office-goers, giving me company. I'm way too late for school.

I take a right turn at the Dashprakash junction and follow the pavement, turning left at the intersection, hoping that neither the headmaster nor my teacher is too upset to make my punishment any more severe than it would be. If a student is more than five minutes late, he is made to wait in the narrow foyer of the headmaster's room. The headmaster then calls the tardy student, and asks him the reason for being late. Only when he is completely satisfied, is the student allowed to go to class. I wonder now even if my best excuse—my critical eye condition—will be enough to get my tardiness condoned. Come to think of it, I might resort to another issue since my eye condition would prompt even more questions.

It's been nearly a month since I went on the pilgrimage to Nattarasankottai, Samayapuram, Chidambaram, and a few other shrines. The plan of visiting these places had seemed tentative at first. Dad as usual had backed out citing that it was the 'peak season' of his business. Ma too would have cancelled the trip, had it not been for her brother agreeing to accompany us.

After endless hours of staring at the expanse of green fields and busy roads from our bus window, we reached Sivagangai. The town earned its place in history as the home of the Marudhu brothers, who had fought against the British. We soon reached the house of my uncle's friend, who had agreed to let us stay at his place. His house would serve as a base camp, from where we would travel to the different temples.

Before entering the precinct of the Kannudaya Nayaki (the Goddess with divine eyes) temple in Nattarasankottai, I was instructed to perform the 'roll on' prayer. I had to lie down on my stomach, wearing nothing but a wet white cloth around my waist, and roll over the entire length of the long granite passage around the sanctum sanctorum until I came back to the spot I had started from. If this wasn't enough, I had to do the exercise on an empty stomach. This ritual would enable me to absorb the divine energy stored in every inch of the temple's floor. It was worth all the discomfort, I was assured, as it would energize my eyes, since the Goddess herself is protector of the eyes.

I lay down, terrified that some of the overzealous devotees might crush me under their heels, but was relieved to find out that there weren't many people in the temple. Propping my chin up on the hard granite, I took one last look at the sanctum sanctorum, and then began rolling myself down the corridor. Fortunately people moved to the side and let me pass, as getting up in the middle of the ritual would break the continuity and thus would not be successful. Every time I turned around, I felt my empty stomach gurgle and I had to swallow back the harsh bile. Calling the ritual difficult would be an understatement, because rolling at a constant speed, without stopping for about half a kilometre, on an empty stomach, would make any heptathlon athlete proud. Yet, despite the rigour, I felt a strange peace and complete absence of fear envelop me. Yes, many might call it a futile exercise, but you'll probably have to be a believer to understand how I felt.

I repeated the same ritual at Samayapuram, a huge shrine of Goddess Mariamman. As soon as we reached Chidambaram though, Uncle Cheenu suggested that we consult an astrologer there. 'He's so good, his predictions are absolutely exact', he said.

We soon found ourselves in the front room of the astrologer's house. It was a 4/4 room with its cement floor concealed under a sprawling blanket and bookshelves brimming with literature on Shastras and astrology. Seated on the blanket, Ma, uncle, and I watched one of the doors open and a scrawny man made an entrance. He clasped his hands to his chest in a gesture of welcome and sat behind a small desk. He asked us for the details of my birth in order to chart out a fresh horoscope and closely studied the squares representing the planetary positions. For the next ten minutes or so, he made notes, splitting his focus between the piece of paper and the notebook he was using to jot down his thoughts.

'There's something wrong with this boy's eyes,' he declared looking up from the notes. My mother and uncle eagerly nodded, while I cast an accusatory glance at my uncle who knew the astrologer quite well. It seemed obvious that he had passed on the information about my condition to him prior to our visit. As the astrologer reeled out more details of my past with amazing accuracy, including the fact that I had been wearing glasses since childhood, it was clear that the astrologer wasn't merely interpreting the planetary positions.

Seemingly enjoying the surprise and awe on the faces of my two companions, he went on to declare that the serious eye problem that I had would soon disappear without a trace, and my stars strongly suggested that I would lead a normal life. I saw my uncle nod and smile many times.

Staying calm in the presence of the astrologer; listening to him reveal tiny nuggets of my life history, was an enormous effort. As soon as we left his place, I turned to my mother and said, 'I'm okay, Ma. My eyes are okay! Please stop dragging me to these places.'

'We're not doing this for you, but for us,' she replied, her eyes turning moist.

'Then, do this without me! I'm not coming along anymore.'

When we returned home, Ma made sure that everything was back to order and routine. I couldn't wait to get back to school again. But there was one more thing left for me to do, I was warned. Raman uncle suggested that we get a second opinion from another ophthalmologist. He helped us get an appointment at one of the city's best eye hospitals only two days after our return from the pilgrimage. Ma was eager that I take a second opinion; and she prayed that it might prove Dr Rakesh's diagnosis a false alarm.

Once more, I had to sit through the painful ordeal of getting my eyes dilated. Irrespective of the medical records I had, the new hospital subjected me to go through all the basic tests once again. A young and attractive female doctor, who I suspected had just walked out of medical school, ushered me towards a telescope-like instrument that had an eyepiece at one end and a stand to rest my chin upon on the other.

'Now... Can you look straight ahead?' I did, but not without noticing that the doctor was adjusting the eyepiece and directing a bright beam of light into my eyes. She stared through the instrument with obvious excitement. At first I felt just a minor disturbance, but as she changed the angles and targeted the light once again into my pupils, the pain grew into severe throbbing.

'Stay like this for a while, okay?' she said, moving towards the door.

She returned a while later with a bunch of doctors not older than herself, who all took turns to examine my eyes. I could see their expressions change from behind the eyepiece I was staring into, but they said nothing in my presence. I realized that my eyes had become a kind of anatomical model for the doctors, who were probably seeing a retina afflicted with genetic degeneration for the first time.

'Your son has all the symptoms of night blindness,' the young doctor said, much to Ma's bafflement. But before she could ask the doctor more questions, I whispered to her that night blindness was one of the symptoms of RP.

So, the second opinion only confirmed Dr Rakesh's diagnosis, and put to rest any lingering doubts that he might have made a mistake. This, without a doubt, was a setback for Ma and the others in my family. If anything, it motivated them more towards finding me a cure. It didn't matter what means they were going to use—allopathy, spiritual, cosmic, or alternative medicine—all they eventually wanted was a solution.

'So... What made you come so late this morning?' I find the headmaster standing before me as I walk into the school gate. There are four other students standing beside me, and yet he picks only me for the drill.

'Sir, there was a heavy traffic jam. It didn't clear out for twenty minutes.'

'Which route do you take, son?'

'I came in from Central, sir.'

'Oh is that so? Then, let me check about its traffic situation with one of our clerks. He takes the same route...'

'But, Sir, this happened just after nine. He...he might have started earlier.'

The headmaster comes close to me. I see that his clean-shaven face is rather chubby, almost childlike, as he smiles at me with sealed lips.

'Okay. I believe you. Let me check the latecomer's register and see if I can send you to your class, which, by the way will end in just twenty minutes,' he says, lifting his wrist and pointing at the dial of his watch.

I run to my classroom, located at the end of the corridor, and then stand at its entrance for one more round of questioning by my teacher. When I am allowed to enter, I rush to my seat and find Balu busy writing down something.

'What's this?'

'It's the portion for half-yearly exams.'

The past few weeks have left me with no time for preparation. The news from Balu has added a new component to the whole thing: terror. With unfamiliar subjects and a long absence from school, I'm clueless as to how I would manage preparations for the half-yearly. For the quarterly exams, I had borrowed and begged for class notes and somehow managed to scrape through. But now? Can I do that again? I am hoping to count on Balu, like before. I'll be doomed, though, if he falls short of the study materials.

The next few days fly by in perusing lessons and copying down notes. I study frantically in my most favourite place at home—the spot near the kitchen where I do all my serious work. It's quiet here after dinner when Ma clears out the dishes and sends off everyone else to bed. Sitting alone, I pore over the bundle of notes with only twittering crickets for company.

I close my eyes and take a deep breath, hoping that the dull throb around my eyes is just an amplified autosuggestion after the gruelling eye examination. When I had first walked into class, my classmates had welcomed me with cold smiles and half-hearted wishes, the kind of welcome reserved for rare visitors and strangers. But I had felt a need, to be a part of their class, to be friends with them. I had cursed myself for having gone on all those meaningless trips to godmen and astrologers, for having lost so much time without my classmates, and ending up feeling alone in the crowd. However, as days passed by, the common crisis of exams revived some of the friendships I thought I had lost forever.

The boys, who had first responded with hesitant hellos, now speak more freely and I find myself slowly becoming friends with some classmates I hardly knew before. I share particular interest for music with Dinesh while I discuss movies with the others. We keep chatting about the latest releases as if the local newspapers are after us for our opinion and reviews.

The exams are soon over without any cause for alarm and it is time for a week-long vacation. As the school ground gets empty after the last exam, Sundar asks us to join him for a movie at the nearby Sangam theatre. We immediately get on our bicycles, ready to go. I sit on the saddle, my favourite position on the bicycle, while the real owner sits behind me as a pillion passenger.

It is unusually hot for late November, and I find the sun somewhat troublesome as we ride over to the theatre. The reflection from the moving vehicles shimmers a little too much in the bright afternoon light, while their contours blur out of focus. I blink to clear away my tears and assume that the discomfort is due to the sun's glare.

As my friends disappear behind the building's rear area to park their bicycles, I notice a long flight of stairs leading to the lobby which seems cool and inviting. Standing in the harsh sun, my eyes are still only half open to escape its glare, and I fail to notice my group rounding in from the rear. One of them clasps my shoulder from behind and shouts 'let's hurry'. We mount the flight of stairs, two at a time, to ensure that we settle in before the movie begins. We brush past a few guys standing in the lobby hoping to buy the last few tickets.

As we turn right, I notice the corridor getting narrower and progressively darker. At first, the blinding sensation seems no different from the eyes taking time to adjust to the darkness. But I note with alarm that I continue to see nothing. The wall of darkness prevails over the bustle of movement and hurrying voices. I then stop moving, which, I realize is the body's natural reaction to total darkness. My knees lock as if it has an auto lock system. I blink continuously in my desperation to ensure that I'm okay and can see. But all I manage is to stare at darkness. My pulse quickens, heart pounds, and sweat streams down my forehead. I want to shut out that one thought which seems to flicker like a danger signal: 'Have I gone blind?... Have I?... Have I!'

An impatient poke at the rib by one of my companions brings back my attention, but my body is still paralyzed with fright and the first experience of realizing what it is to be blind. The boy pulls me towards the entrance and that momentary physical contact seems to relieve my stress a bit. I tentatively follow the moving figure ahead, realizing that we're now closer to the row of seats.

'Sit down... This's your seat.' Sundar's instruction prompts me to turn right and hunker down. The plush leather seat feels cool and relieving, but terror comes back as I'm no longer distracted by physical movement. Holding my forehead in my palms, I try not to cry. But tears roll down along with helpless prayers: 'God! Oh please, God! Let me see, please let me see.'

As I open my eyes, the grey silhouettes of many heads against the bright screen zooms in gradually like the opening shot of a movie. I take a few deep breaths to get rid of the tension and realize, with a smile, how good it is to see. 'Yeah… it does feel good after all', I murmur with relief. Sundar, seated to my left, squeezes my hand.

'What the hell? Did you just go in a trance while walking in?' he whispers.

'No… There are a lot of people around and I was looking at the screen.'

Relief turns into pleasure as I watch the colourful picture of a waterfall, the yellow blouse and black half sari on the heroine. I can see…really…'

'But I thought…you had some trouble walking…' Sundar starts again, but is interrupted by a loud burst of music. Time for some song and dance. Our conversation will have to wait. It's time to immerse ourselves in the fantastic world of the movie. The terror that had consumed my mind some minutes ago soon recedes into oblivion.

As I turn into my street against the setting sun, I'm still in two minds about discussing the theatre incident with Ma. I know it's important to disclose whatever I experience with family and close ones so that they at least know to what extent I need assistance in doing ordinary day to day things. Perhaps Ma will talk to Dr Rakesh and ascertain if this has got anything to do with RP But this will also mean that Ma's effort to treat the condition through alternative medicinal methods is certainly not working to our satisfaction, and I'm sure this will bother her a great deal. In the end, it's not worth the heartache. I decide that it would be best to keep the incident to myself, at least for now.

But every time I think of it, I feel like sharing it with someone just to get rid of the fear and terror it brings. I become speechless the moment my mind drifts towards those dreadful few minutes, as if to remind me that the sense of normality around me is nothing more than an illusion. I need a few deep breaths and positive affirmations to get out of the fright. In those moments, I wish life could have been much simpler. Probably it would be, if Ma hadn't cried in Dr Rakesh's clinic or if I hadn't asked what was wrong. If I didn't know how terrifying my condition is, I would perhaps not take those momentary difficulties as reminders of the condition that is dragging me into permanent darkness.

SIX

The Unseen Shadow

The impatient horns of traffic, the insistent whistles of trains pulling in and out of the Central, and the shrill chirruping of sparrows—the symphony of a city that wakes up early—drags me out of sleep. School is reopening today, and I can't wait to meet my new friends and share a joke or two with them before the classes start.

I may have missed my classmates but I never really missed the lessons for even a single moment. The jokes, the bantering, and the good times spent with my friends is the only thing that keeps me sane, and I intend to make it last as long as I can.

It has been more than a week since the cinema incident, and thankfully, it hasn't occurred again. Of course, I haven't been to a similar dark place again either, but I am still convinced that it was an aberration—at least I desperately hope it is.

To get rid of bad memories, I try a simple technique I had been taught earlier. I sit on the mattress, close my eyes and visualize what had happened at the theatre. In my imagination, I 'trap' the memory in a bottle, watch it condense into a smaller, insignificant image, and then see myself tossing it into a trash can. But any illusion that I may have gotten rid of the condition retreats in a hurry the moment I've doubts about my own vision. If something blurs or goes hazy for a second or two, a chill runs down my spine. The terrifying minutes I had spent trying to break open the wall of darkness, listening to voices and movement around me, comes crowding back with startling clarity. My body goes rigid the way it did then and knees auto lock, even when I fight to tune myself out of that memory.

Yes, the theatre incident could have been an aberration, but it has planted a perpetual sense of doubt about what I see and how I see it. And that doubt flares up each time I naturally fail to notice something. Even if it is something as ordinary as a stone that I may unknowingly stumble upon. If ever there's someone who can't believe his own eyes, it's me. It's unlikely that life would be ever normal.

'This is absurd!' I reprimand myself, as a sudden defiance replaces the uncertain fear. 'I can't live like this. I can't allow this fear to take over my life!'

I take a deep breath, close my eyes, and then open

them with such force that in that instant my eyes can clearly see everything. I consult the watch and realize it's time to get ready and get going.

Time flies; here I am, looking at the distant towers of Madras Central on my right, and watching the hands of its huge clock crawl past 9 am. I'm waiting at the bus stop, standing beneath a large tree, watching the torrent of traffic rush past. Number 20 soon arrives, the same bus I take to school every day. I get onto its footboard and feel relieved to find an empty seat. I sit, turn my head, and watch the clock tower and its big face recede into the distance. What a blessing it is to see clearly, I think to myself.

If meditation and visualization would somehow help me sidestep reality, this belief is proven wrong the very afternoon. It's nearly an hour after school and it is time to board the bus back home. Anxious that I might be late, I quicken my pace across the empty corridor, turn right, and start descending the flight of stairs. I must have come down three or four steps when, in a split second, the stairway below goes hazy as my sight fails me again. Unable to control the speed of my descent, I topple down, banging my right elbow on the staircase, turning and rolling over, and finally falling on the floor with a violent thud. During the fall, the books and notebooks I am holding, slip off my grasp and slide across the stairway; while my glasses fly off and crash into the railing.

By the time two watchmen and a few students run to my rescue, I realize that I have become a total wreck. I hold on to them and try rather gingerly to stand on my feet. My neatly combed hair is nothing more than a tangle, shirt is crumpled and dirty, and eyes are all teary like a child. 'What have I done to deserve this?' The question echoes in my mind, and I have only that helpless trembling for an answer because none of this makes sense. If everyone really thinks that this is the result of some unknown sin, as many godmen and people seem to suggest, I'd like to know how serious a sin is that. Had I known, I would have probably bartered an arm or a leg to retain my eyes because I do realize their importance. But I guess this situation is such that I've to simply go through it without questioning. Like a trapped animal, my helplessness only triggers resentment against everything from people around me to providence. What loving God would let one of his creations struggle like this?

I want to assure the anxious folks around me that I feel fine, but walk away in silence realizing that the painful attempt to speak would only keep them to me and not away from me. Still reeling from the shock and pain, I can't bring myself even to care about my messy appearance. I walk towards the gate, not bothering to wipe the tears. Memory of missing those steps, play repeatedly in my mind like the footage of a catastrophe, making me relive the incident again and again. Will this be the last time my eyes fail me at an inopportune moment or will it happen again? I try recollecting Dr Rakesh's diagnosis to find something which would point to the momentary lapse of my eyesight. But I don't have answers to any of those questions. The fact is that I don't know much about anything. It's hardly comforting to go through life with a condition that creates questions and doubts and gives little room for awareness or preparation. The urge to shout in sheer fright and anger is too hard to resist as I trail my vacant gaze towards the busy traffic outside the gate.

'Trust yourself, goddammit! Trust yourself,' I order myself in a snarly whisper that escapes my biting teeth. 'And trust your eyes! Accidents happen with everyone. Don't you know that?'

Beyond the open gate, traffic flows; the sheer energy of it seems like the rush of blood through the arteries of an active city. It's a relief that I can still see those cars and motorbikes plying about on either side of the road. I continue to watch until the trembling stops and memory of the fall fades away into oblivion.

The best person to answer these persistent questions is Dr Rakesh. He can tell me if those blurs are just aberrations or if they are the opening salvo of a long and tortuous battle with RP.

Dr Rakesh, in fact, is the only person who can fully comprehend the complexity of my condition. So, I'm back at his clinic that very evening to find out. This place, with the creamy walled waiting room and the bustle of patients walking in and out, offers the kind of comfort I rarely find elsewhere. The long wait for my turn seems like a sign of reassurance that things won't be as bad as I fear. I smile at the thought and squeeze Ma's hand and she smiles back. It's a treat, like sunshine on a cloudy day, because Ma rarely smiles these days.

Dr Rakesh examines my eyes. As he projects the shaft of light into my iris, I find him look glum. There isn't even a half-hearted attempt to smile. This probably shows his feelings about the present condition of my retinas. I look at him, half expecting a request to step out again, but that doesn't come this time. How comforting? Instead, he motions me to the chair facing him and points to a picture on the table.

'The retina, as you perhaps know, has millions of light-sensing cells on its surface that capture light and images, which is then converted into electrical pulses and sent to the brain through the optic nerves,' Dr Rakesh explains, pointing to the picture that shows a rather reddish tissue.

'The defective gene prevents blood and oxygen from reaching these light-detecting cells and triggers a slow process of blindness. How soon or how late this will happen differs from patient to patient. You see the slight hint of dark blue here?' he points at the next picture, which has dark blue spots scattered across the retina's red region.' These dark blue spots are the decayed cells that cannot perceive light.'

Dr Rakesh then looks at me with a grave expression and says, 'The only thing we can do is to hope for the best.'

'What do you mean by hoping for the best doctor?' I ask him knowing well where this conversation is headed to, but unable to control the urge to hear it from him.

'Well...', he sighs tilting his head towards the ceiling with closed eyes. Looking again at the picture, he points to the dark spots on the bright red retina and says, 'These slowly spread and in the end your retina would turn almost completely dark blue. I am just hoping it doesn't happen at least for now.'

I stare at the picture and realize that this is the monster in the mirror moment for me. The monster, so to say, is a blotch of tissue that determines my disability status in the future. It's hardly comforting that it would happen slowly and I must consider myself lucky that I may have a few more years before going completely blind.

'What about the treatment?' I ask in a queasy voice that hardly conceals discomfort.

Dr Rakesh moistens his lips anxiously, looking for the right words. 'There is no treatment for this,' he finally says. 'Research is going on, of course, in many places in the world. But it's highly unlikely that there will be a breakthrough anytime soon.'

'But why me, doctor? Why did I get this condition?'

The lengthening silence only accentuates the awkwardness. Thankfully, Dr Rakesh breaks the silence and says, 'Consanguinity.' He launches into another detailed explanation. 'It's a kind of genetic similarity usually found between a closely related male and a female. An identical weaker gene in them could possibly express itself as a disability in the offspring.'

I sit up straight and notice comprehension dawning on Ma's face. 'Doctor, do you mean to say that I've got this condition because...because my parents are related?'

'Nothing is certain, but yes that is a very strong possibility.'

Knowing about an unpalatable reality isn't the same as reconciling or dealing with it. Consanguinity may not have changed anything Dr Rakesh had to say about my eye condition, but it certainly makes my heart ache more severely than before. It's now an effort to wake up in the morning, get ready and stumble through the busy road towards the bus stop, and get to school.

Even during the classes, I can't help drifting off and chewing over the latest disclosure. With school and my own feelings, I'm too cocooned in my own world to have space or time for any conversation with my parents. But judging Ma's expression when we left the clinic, I'm pretty sure that the knowledge that they caused my condition, though unwittingly, is enough to make them feel extremely guilty. Be that as it may, I believe there is no reason for them to confuse this with the 'sin' that astrologers yap about all the time. A defective or weak gene is nothing more than what it is and we shouldn't lose sleep over its biological permutations and combinations. If God didn't want me to go through it, I wouldn't be wrestling with it now and if he did, I'm too powerless to reverse it. But I guess we have visited too many astrologers and allowed ourselves to be conquered by the 'sin' theory. A part of it has got to do with the fact that my family and relatives believe in such things and try applying half-baked theories into challenging situations to arrive at potentially alarming conclusions.

So the stir caused by Dr Rakesh's latest revelation isn't really a shock for the family, but it certainly caught us off guard. As they say, we're all experts in hindsight. Now, it's time for the experts in shastras and Vedic texts to question if a union between my parents should have been allowed. Since we learnt about it later, it didn't really appear like just a cerebral exercise or something to satisfy the curiosity of a bunch of people, but it was rather a heated exchange in which fingers were pointed at both my father's and mother's family for having contributed the 'weaker' gene. Needless to say, such arguments bring no good except further lowering the family's morale.

At the time of my parent's wedding, no one had thought that a marriage within such genealogical proximity would prove to be a problem. In fact, it was a common practice for us to marry cousins and nieces to ensure familial bonding. This way we didn't have to include a stranger into either our family tree or will. It never occurred to anyone that marriages like these were one of the main causes of genetic defects. Also, they had no way of knowing that Retinitis Pigmentosa affects more people in South India, probably because consanguinity is more common there than in the Northern region.

For a neighbourhood which has to contend with nothing more than births, deaths, and an occasional capture of a petty thief, the news of a boy grappling with a mysterious eye condition caused quite a stir.

It was munched in conversations with a lot more gusto. The usual bearer of local news, the feeder of the rumour mill—Shantamma—the old woman who delivers the monthly allocation of rice, sugar, and kerosene to half a dozen households, was suspected of spreading this news. If gossipmongers were to be believed, it became obvious to everyone that there was a strong suspicion of me going blind.

Walking along the street, I'm conscious that I'm attracting more and more attention. Folks, who used to throw a wary glance in my direction, now openly gawk at me, as if they have no hesitations to stop me in the middle of the road, turn me around and check if I can still see. There are a few genuinely sympathetic looks, of course, but I mostly see either curiosity or contempt.

'How come most of it is raw?' I ask a shopkeeper at the vegetable market one day, as I pick out tomatoes for Ma.

'They are not raw. Look properly—or are you really going blind?'

My face turns red and I tell her, 'You've got no right to talk to me that way. I'll never buy from your shop again.'

'As if I care! Throw your measly coins at someone who can tolerate your rudeness,' she snarls. I leave the shop livid, embarrassed, and somewhat wounded. 'That was just a casual remark. She can't possibly know about my eyes,' I try telling myself, but in vain.

'We heard that you're going blind?' I am asked another day at the barbershop down the street. The barber is a burly man in his 40s. The question is blunt and sudden. 'No. Not really. I have a condition that could possibly lead to blindness, but even the doctors aren't sure about it.' I see a wry smile on his face, and I can imagine the rumour mill spinning fast and furiously behind my back.

'So, are you really going blind then? Is that what Ma and Dad are worried about?' Arjun, my little brother, asks me as we return home from the barber's shop. Arjun is three years younger than me. He and my nine-year-old sister, Lakshmi live with our family, while my brother Eshwar, who is four years my junior, stays with Raman uncle.

Arjun's thin hand trembles when it clutches my elbow. I look into his agitated face and realize that I have never seen him that pale. We always had a little rivalry between us. Since childhood, we have constantly hit at each other's sore spots and got on each other's nerves, but I guess things have changed now. No more pranks.

I turn and look into his eyes and speak softly. 'You heard what I told the barber, right? It's a condition, a kind of a defect, but I'll be alright.'

Arjun continues to stare at me as if he is trying to look through me. We resume walking towards home, letting the silence do the talking.

'If you wear thicker glasses, would it help?' Arjun asks me suddenly.

'I think so.'

The knowledge of my condition and possible blindness among my neighbours and family isn't surprising or entirely unexpected. What is unexpected though is the crash landing of my once brilliant future in the eyes of these folks. While I'm still struggling to grapple with the idea of disability, the suggestion, though subtle, that disability equals incompetence or worthlessness, isn't quite uplifting and is indeed hard to digest.

'Oh, he's really focused,' beams an aunt, who has a son about my age, as she speaks of his educational exploits. 'We're sure he'll end up doing pretty much what he wants to.'

Usually this kind of remark in a family gathering never went unchallenged by Ma, but now the thought of it fill her eyes with tears.

'How's your son coping?' asks another relative,

and in no time the mood quickly turns from celebration to a sombre analysis of my condition.

'He's doing fine. Too young, perhaps, to realize the seriousness of the situation,' Ma responds, trying hard to smile.

And thus, just like that, I seem to have relinquished my place in the family's list of promising children to occupy an altogether new status—the most unfortunate one.

Nevertheless, not all in our family circle are so callous or ignorant. A few who are genuinely concerned about my condition and the impact it has on my family, visit us with the holy ashes and kumkums from temples. It's a touching gesture which makes me feel like a part of a larger community. Of course, they also bring with them therapy techniques which they believe would work. Some of them also suggest recipes with vegetables that could have a healing effect.

Unsurprisingly, I find more 'healing' foods included in Ma's daily cooking, especially greens. Someone suggests that I eat ponnankani or water amaranth, a variety of green that promises to improve eyesight. Ma also regularly cooks drumstick greens, which is both tasty and healthy for the eyes. I can't say the same about many other concoctions and 'brews' of vegetables and flowers that she makes.

Ma regularly concocts a solution of milk and drumstick flowers, which I have to swallow on an empty stomach. The blandness stirs in a strong sense of nausea. After taking the full-course of this vile liquid for nearly a fortnight, I am given a new concoction. This time it is a mixture of milk with nandiyavattai or crape jasmine. The tiny, pure white flowers are a treat to the eyes, but drinking them with milk isn't nearly as pleasant. Even after I drink these herbal concoctions, the taste keeps lingering on my tongue for an unbearably long time. I have to then rush to the toilet and flush it all out.

SEVEN

A Fugitive from Fear

At first, the figure stepping out from the classroom, down the corridor, seems 'normal'. He seems to be just another boy in white and khaki uniform. I see him standing just outside the class, dressed in immaculate white uniform and spotless shoes. His face is glowing and chubby. It is boyish but there's something wrong with it. Yes, it's his eyes. They make his otherwise attractive face look strange and bizarre.

His eyes are completely white. Is there no iris within them? I look at him again, the familiar hum of fear vibrating loudly in my ears. I realize that he's blind. I try to calm down, but with no effect. The boy unfolds a white cane and places his hand onto the arm of the person accompanying him. He is probably his father. The sight terrifies me, and my heart pushes away the most natural feeling of empathy that threatens to enter it. 'He is not what I want to be!' The boy is both a peek into my future and an embodiment of my present fears. I turn away from him and look towards the distant playground. I see a group of juniors playing football.

'That's Krish', Balu says as he stops beside me and watches the student walk past us.

'Quite a bright chap they say. He's in the economics stream. Don't you feel inspired seeing someone like that?' he asks admiringly.

'Yes I am', I whisper. It is a sinking feeling, but I try convincing my mind to expel the image of the boy from it. Then, for half an hour I make constant self-affirmations that I won't become like him.

Two days later, as I walk past the headmaster's room, I'm stopped by a soft voice: 'Excuse me.'

It's the boy again. I stand speechless for a while, fighting the surge of panic and not answering him. I want to brush my fears aside and comfort him; tell him that I am there to help, make him feel better and ease his frustrations, but that is easier said than done.

'I'm... How can I help you?' I manage to blurt out.

'Something fell down from my pocket. Sounded

like metal. I guess it's a coin. Could you pleae get that for me?'

My rational mind tries hard to explain that each one of us, blind or sighted, needs help and that's exactly what I'm doing, just helping another person in need. His blindness has no connection with me, my condition, or my own future. But the trouble with any deep, inexplicable emotion is that it is irrational and as such cannot be smoothed over by rational talk.

'I sense you're in a hurry to leave. I'm sorry, I didn't realize that,' his voice is kind and regret is genuine.

'No, it's alright.' I notice, as I speak, that my own voice is cold and mournful. I hate myself for who I've become at that moment. His generosity makes me feel ashamed of myself. Yet I'm unable to ward off the strange fear that grips me every time I think of blindness.

'I'm sorry. I should have answered sooner,' I admit, placing the coin onto his outstretched palm.

'It's okay. It happens when you aren't used to blind people,' he consoles me and walks away.

I can't quite stop thinking of blindness, in spite of the streaming cold sweat on my forehead each time I do so. What does it mean or how does it feel?

What happens to someone who goes blind? Does he see only darkness? Questions like these rumble in my head like a motor engine and I suspect that it's much harder to control such thoughts because of the kind of feelings it inspires. I gulp down the herbal tablets and powders with full determination. Desperation would be the right word. But whatever it may be, never before did I feel so strongly about something or had the urge to run a mile away from blindness if I could help it. It's uplifting even to hold those vile tasting liquids and tablets and to believe that they would stop the rot in my retina. A renewed sense of belief fills my heart each time I lift those bottles and unwrap the pill cases. As if I've already started to run away from blindness, I sink into the routine of school lessons, medicines, and temple visits, and the optimism seems to grow. I'm happy that I'm no longer rocked by those confidence-battering momentary blurs. Going through the routine is relieving, and being able to see without the blurs is reassuring. Life can't get any better!

One evening, I once again find mother sitting in the

kitchen, seemingly crestfallen. Dr Rakesh, it seems, wants to test Arjun, Eshwar, and Lakshmi's eyes for Retinitis Pigmentosa.

'He says it's just a precaution,' Ma said. 'It'll be good if the doctor is able to confirm that nothing's wrong with them. God, I really hope there's nothing wrong with them.'

The next morning, seated in my school's classroom, I keep thinking of the test that's being done to my brothers and sister at that very moment. My lips tremble slightly, as I murmur a prayer for their well-being. I start to grow more impatient with every passing minute. Though thinking about the result of the examination is tiresome, it's harder to divert my mind towards other activities. So it's a blessing when the final bell for the day rings. I sprint to the bus stop and head towards home. I press the call bell more than once before Ma unbolts the door.

'What happened? What did the doctor say?'

Ma walks back inside quickly as if she doesn't want to face me. Why? It feels as if my heart is about to sink. The situation stirs those memories that I never want to recall. 'Oh dear God...not any more of that...' I tell myself gripping the door's handle with extra force. Mustering my strength, I bolt back the door and follow Ma to the kitchen.

'What happened, Ma? Are they alright?'

'Yes they are,' she says, turning off the gas stove just before the boiling milk overflows from the brim of the vessel. I take a deep breath and find myself washed over with relief and exhaustion. 'You should have told me immediately,' I tell her impatiently as she looks at the steaming milk.

When I return from school one afternoon, I find one of the neighbours speaking to my mother. As I remove my footwear, I realize that the women haven't heard my footsteps and are unaware of my presence.

'It's so sad that an eye problem has affected your son,' the woman says.

'Yes. We never expected something as severe as this eye condition would afflict him. He has always been a healthy child and even now he remains healthy except for this problem,' Ma replys.

'What's the point anyway? He'll still be useless to you. At least God has been so kind to leave you with two more boys,' the woman says, and perhaps notices Ma's livid expression a little too late.

'Let's not forget that you are speaking about

my son! Besides, he'll never go blind, whatever the doctors say. He'll come out safe and will succeed in life.' Ma rarely raises her voice but when she does, it's sharp like a sabre.

I quickly enter the hall, ignoring the awkward expression on the face of our guest, drop my bag inside the room, and inform my mother that I'll be out for some time.

'Useless!' This again is a monster in the mirror moment; only that I'm seeing a different facet of that image now. First, it was the dented image of a boy who once had a brilliant future ahead of him. Now his status of being worthless on account of his impending blindness is confirmed. I don't know why people think that a person going blind must necessarily be useless. Maybe it is because the society confuses a person's physical weakness with mental ineptitude, or perhaps it likes to take the easy route of portraying a person with disability as 'useless' when it actually should be taking initiatives to help him stand on his feet. Well...I don't actually have to go blind to find this out. 'Useless', I smirk as I walk towards Mr JRK's house and mount the steps. I pause to catch my breath before climbing more stairs. The words, and what it meant, still hurt me.

Mr JRK's family has been our friend ever since my parents moved into the neighbourhood in 1972. What began as a neighbourly acquaintance grew into a strong friendship over the years to such an extent that our families can now count on each other for support in times of trouble.

In his mid-70s now, Mr JRK has a perfectly round face, framed by salt and pepper hair that is always combed back neatly and seems to grey rather slowly. Along with a warm smile that immediately endears him to people, Mr JRK also has a pair of sharp, piercing eyes that can always catch a bluff.

I find Mr JRK on the vast, open terrace of his house.

'Looks like you had a fight at home,' he says, his eyes fixed on the busy street below.

'Not a fight,' I reply, unsurprised by his perceptive observation. 'I'm just upset about something I heard.'

He listens to my incoherent ranting about the woman who thinks I'm useless and about the meddling barber and the rude vegetable seller.

'What kind of a world is this? It treats a person with a challenging condition as a subject of juicy gossip! Instead of supporting the person and his family, all that they show is insensitivity and callousness. They don't realize the gravity of anything unless it happens to them.'

'Son, the world is an unfair place. You'll do well if you remember this. Now, I'm not asking you to put up with its unfairness. Fight it, resist it with all the strength you have, but don't lull yourself into thinking that the world is fair,' he adds.

I remain quiet, crest fallen.

'Stop pitying yourself,' he snaps. 'You'll only end up inflicting pain on yourself and others.'

Having spent many years in his company, I know that Mr JRK isn't impervious to my pain. I also know that his sharp tone is only meant to wrench me out of my rage. Of course, it has its intended effect.

EIGHT

The Setback and a Chance

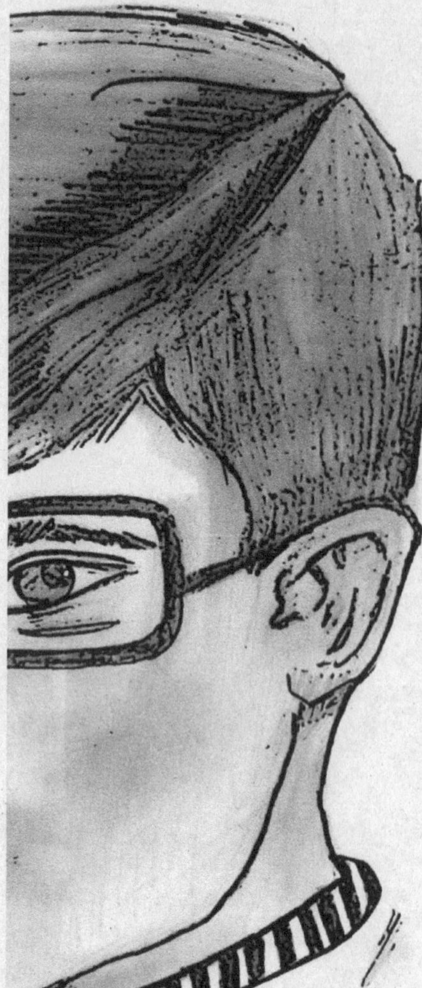

It's the summer holidays of 1989, and I'm almost done with the temple visits and appointments with therapists. My last visit is to Tirupati, where I find myself washing my body in the intolerably cold waters of the temple tank at 3 am in preparation for yet another roll on ritual. Fifty other devotees slosh along in their wet dhotis, sprawled on the cold granite of the temple corridor, and start to roll on the floor along with me. I like the company of people, but this is too much of a crowd.

Arriving home, I look at the face staring back at me in the mirror and realize how the hairless head has altered my identity, much to my dismay. The shining head, where there used to be neatly combed and parted hair, makes me look stupid. I will have to put up with it, if my efforts of petitioning God were to ever stand a chance of success. I have disfigured myself, not out of my love for God, but only as a means of bartering my hair in return for his blessings. I've stuck to my side of the bargain, and now can only hope that God sticks to his.

Thankfully it is still May and I don't have to think about school since it would reopen only three weeks later. Yet, it seems strange to be completely unaware of the results of my higher secondary exams, which should be out any time now. I remember how, in the past, I used to feel extremely nervous, when the postcard with the results used to arrive at home. Now of course, I have bigger things to worry about.

As soon as I finish lunch, hungry and exhausted from my trip, I hear the doorbell ring. I open it to find Balu standing there, expressionless. At first I think this is because of my hairless head. But Balu stonewalls my sheepish grin, and walks in with a taut face. He neither responds to my warm welcome nor to my offer of coffee and savouries. After perfunctory greetings to the older folks, Balu pulls me into the other room.

'I've been trying to contact you for two days. The results are out!'

We look at each other.

'Oh is it?' I say with nervous anticipation.

'All of us have passed...'

'Oh real...'

Balu cuts me short and says, 'Except two people.

And, I hate to say this...but...you're one of them.'

Balu lowers his head, more in discomfort for having to deliver the news, which, I should say, isn't completely unexpected. But I now feel that failure can taste as bitter as any of those vile liquids that the therapists had administered. Balu knows that I'm not someone who can take failure too well, especially if it is in exams, in which I have never failed before.

'You mean...I've failed?' I ask, not wanting to believe it. Balu nods slightly, apparently lost in thoughts.

In the ensuing silence, I let the disappointment sink in. This could be a setback. In the race to secure my future, before blindness engulfs my eyes, losing one year could prove to be costly. I'd certainly regret the loss if I fail to reach a position in life where I'll have a job and enough money to improve my condition. The present failure has made my future a bit more uncertain than ever before. A familiar feeling of fear envelopes me, shaking off all the strength I am left with. No, I'm not mourning my failure. Marks and results won't change anything, but I can't say the same about losing one year of my life. A pang of regret hits me when I realize that I'll no longer have the same classmates.

Having delivered the dose of bad news, after some time Balu's tensed face slowly changes into a relaxing smile. He becomes cheerful, regaling me with funny stories. But that goes little in the way of defusing the grim reality. I play along nonetheless, nodding and smiling in all the right places, while contemplating on the best course of action that can be taken. Should I give up studies for a while and focus on the therapies as Ma and the others in my family have suggested? Or should I begin afresh? What will happen if I actually go blind?

'This must be really painful for you,' Balu says, observing my feeble smiles.

I cover my sweat-damp face and close my eyes, not knowing whether I should cry or put up a brave face as Mr JRK had suggested.

'Hey, are you alright?' Balu, who seemed like a mature and strong adult a while ago, now behaves like a worried little school boy as he gets up from his chair, bends down before me, and pats my shoulder. 'What's wrong with you? Tell me!'

I ignore him and take a few deep breaths. 'I thought you were going to faint,' he says patting my back. And then he gives me advice, words that, I'm sure, someone has told him before. 'You've just failed in the exam, not in life. Try taking this as a stepping stone towards success.'

'I'm fine,' I whisper. 'This is just upsetting. I thought I'd pass, you know.'

'Don't worry. Things will soon be fine.'

'Right,' I smile. Staying 'normal' and being 'fine' are after all the goals of my inner battle; something Balu has no chance of knowing.

'Being a failure isn't the way people begin their journey towards adulthood,' I confide in Mr JRK during one of my evening visits. I snap my fingers and say, 'No one at home seems to care. I've failed and a year of my life is gone, just like that!'

I am seated in Mr JRK's cosy bedroom. The overcast sky has stopped my elderly neighbour from taking a walk on the terrace as he usually does.

'Failure can sometimes be helpful,' he says, reclining on a huge wooden cot that occupies most of the space in the room. His eyes are closed and he is gently tapping his chin with his right index finger. 'It makes you take a step back and get a fresh perspective on life.'

'The only perspective I get, sir, is that my life is quickly going downhill. Everyone at home seems to think that I can make it up if I ensure my eyesight is stable. But no one really seems to understand that all this, crazy treatment and astrology, has cost me one whole year of my life! This will surely hurt me the most when I go blind.'

'What makes you think you'll go blind? And how are you sure that the medicines won't work? You've just lost one year because you focused on your eyesight rather than studies. It's alright. Just think about how you can move forward.'

For the next few nights, the bulb above the wooden beam flickers constantly and the consistent chirp of crickets fill my ears. There's no exam to prepare or any study roster to maintain, but I need some time alone to think. Apparently, I can make up for the lost year by appearing as a private candidate for the public service exam, which I could have done had I passed. The shortcut to compensate for the lost year came as a suggestion from one of Ma's friends. The other choice, of course, is getting back to school and beginning the first year. Strange as it may sound, this choice appeals to me much more because it would give me a chance to wear a uniform, forge new friendships, and have all the fun that I had missed out in the last year. I may have failed the first time, but I'm sure I won't fail again. This is the assurance I'm prepared to give Ma—and to myself—to be back at school for a second stint.

However, as I turn off the light and feel the darkness fill the space around me, I can't help but think how things will turn out if I were to go blind. Will this decision be wrong? I toss and turn on the bed, not able to make up my mind one way or the other.

NINE

The Illusion of Normalcy

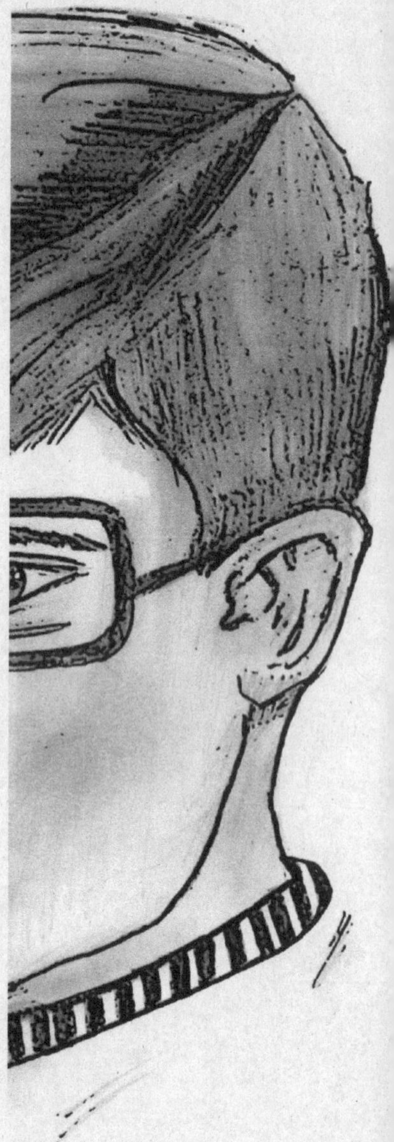

It has taken me a few days to think and carefully consider what option to go for. Appearing as a private candidate in the public service exams might be a smarter move, but I know very well that success will not be guaranteed even then. After all, I couldn't learn my first year lessons well, and as a private candidate, I may not have the luxury of learning lessons at school. Also, it's good to belong somewhere. I believe that would do a world of good to my confidence, battered and fragile as it is.

So looking at the present circumstances, however I analyse it, continuing school and repeating my first year seems like a better option. Of course, it needs a bit of persuasion for Ma to understand my logic and give her consent.

'I never had a chance at passing the exams. I am still not very familiar with the subjects. It's better that I go back and learn everything again.' There's a bit of accusation, frustration, and a little pleading in my tone, as I argue my case with Ma one evening. I still have a week to pay the fees and join school, but for me it's either now or never.

'You can learn the second year lessons at home and then appear for your exams as a private candidate,' Ma waves her hands dramatically as she returns my impatient stares. The milk cooker whistles in the kitchen at that inopportune moment, distracting her from the discussion.

'You'll certainly save time that way and then it'll be easy to continue the treatment,' she says as she comes out of the kitchen, wiping her wet hands on the border of her saree.

'There you are, back again at where we started. If I am busy taking the treatments, when will I get the time to study? Who will teach me?'

The argument went back and forth for a while before I could tell Ma, though in a convoluted way, that I needed to be familiar with the lessons to take the exams privately. She softened her tone and said, 'Okay... I get it. But I'd like you to be committed to the treatment and I certainly don't want you to exert yourself.' I nodded firmly, happy to know that I have her support.

The familiar classroom seems relieving despite seeing unknown faces of students occupying the desks where once my friends sat. Well, at least the teachers, textbooks, and rules of the school haven't changed. Seated in my usual place, watching the classroom fill in for the first day's class, I feel an overwhelming sense of gratitude, not just towards Ma, but also towards life in general. No matter how bad the situation is, there's always something to thank life for...always. Life always gives us a second chance for a fresh beginning; to get things right. I'm also glad that I've been given the chance to realize that my condition hasn't completely taken away my passion to succeed.

The second innings can't be any better as my vision never felt so good before, strengthening my resolve to make the most of the given opportunity. Thankfully, RP hasn't pulled the rug from under my feet as it did a few months ago. True to my words, I pop pills, swallow liquids, and hope that they will work. I burn the midnight oil to ensure that I have good grades to justify my chance. Undoubtedly, it's all going fine, at least for now.

Getting a reprieve isn't the same as getting the monkey off the back. It's always there even in its absence, and I can't have felt its hideous presence at a time worse than this. It's just a few months after the quarterly tests. I am ascending the steps of the big subway across the Poonamallee High Road. Up ahead is the uneven, vendor-encroached path towards Madras Central. I head into the bright, orange afternoon light that reflects on everything from the grey walls to the colourful vehicles zooming down the road. The traffic is at its noisy best and the hawkers chime in, selling their wares with shouts and screams. For a while, nothing looks different and I have no reason to discontinue walking. But when I blink, as I always do whenever I step into bright light, I notice the edges of objects blurring. It seems as if I can and can't see at the same time. The haze obscures every object in my view and follows my gaze like a faint shadow. After standing still for some time and blinking continuously, the darkness disappears and I continue walking again.

The blur returns a few more times when I walk in the school corridors and across the open ground. It jolts me out of comfort and makes me blink in panic. Of course, my vision feels normal whenever I blink, but it's much harder to dispel the persisting doubts and fears. While walking on a shadowy pavement, I halt suddenly when I see a large iron pillar across the footpath. But I realize, with embarrassment, that it's a shadow. I blink again and again, feeling better when I see things as they are, but nothing feels alright in those unnerving few seconds.

Two summers back, I learnt how to ride a bicycle on the dusty roads of Virudhachalam, my mother's hometown. Though my parents refused to buy me and Arjun a bicycle of our own, I often borrowed one from my friends. Cycling around the busy roads of Madras is certainly liberating. When I deftly manoeuvre my bike between two stationary cars and pass through them with absolute precision, I feel confident about myself. During such moments, I can even believe that the haziness in my eyesight is but the result of a paranoid mind.

In school, I have even tried my hand at cricket. Every time I move my feet, lift hands, and press my wrist down to strike the cherry-red ball coming at me, I feel the same surge in confidence. It feels so refreshing to be on my own and to be able to do things without letting fear cloud my mind.

But I should have known better. Reinforcing ego over a fragile retina is more complicated than it seems because when the condition chooses to show up, it diminishes all my confidence. That's how it felt when I once took my stance on a seemingly regular game of cricket. I looked for the ball, its reddish glint in the afternoon sun, and raised my willow bat to strike it. But instead, I felt a heavy thump on the forehead, which made me topple on the ground, breathless. I was hit by a delivery that was shorter than I had expected. All I could see were bright flashes of light and dark blotches. Was it because of my weakening eyesight? I don't know.

I came back to senses after water was splashed on my face. I could see the anxious faces of a few schoolmates standing around. I winced when I touched the painful bump and wasn't sure if my eyes were moist in response to the pain or the dent to my confidence that felt even worse. 'He bowled a beamer,' a student whispered in my ears. 'Someone in the team came up with the idea of bowling a beamer at you. I told them it's dangerous. This is just an informal six-a-side match, but they didn't listen.'

Holding the bat again seems quite difficult. Of course, the handle fits quite nicely between my curled fingers when I grip it, but I tremble when I attempt a shot. What if I miss the ball again? What if? When fear clouds my mind, there's no room for joy and no place for sports. Giving up anything you feel passionate about is tough, but when things no longer seem the usual, it's better to let go of it. A part of me wants to continue with the cycling because I enjoy the leather saddle and the smooth grip of the handlebar. I also love the quicksilver movement around heavy vehicles. But I can't do it anymore, not with the doubt and an unsteady hand. In moments like these, my condition isn't like darkness eclipsing the moon, but it seems more like a giant vacuum cleaner sucking life out of my existence.

I don't completely miss the game because I can always rely on television whenever I want to watch it. I feel good that at one time I did have a chance to play on the ground. But I do feel sad at times. Sensing the forlorn look on my face one day, one of my uncles dragged me to watch a local game. Never before did I feel so elated. Throughout the match, I hooted with a bunch of guys watching the game. Yes...I'm thankful that I can see and want to see for the rest of my life.

Sleep, after the accident on the cricket ground, is light and fretful. When I eventually doze off, fear grips my subconscious mind and throws up images in the form of a nightmare.

I am on a busy street. I can hear the shouts of hawkers, the noise of people, talking, laughing, and walking around me. It seems like an unfamiliar place, almost like a foreign country. But then I see a man in the crowd...a face that I know. There's something familiar about him. I try looking at his eyes, but find them obscured by a large pair of dark glasses. He walks slowly along with the crowd. His stride seems hesitant. He's holding a white stick in his hand. I cover my ears and scream *Blind*! *Blind*!

Terrified, I sit up. My heart is pounding and sweat is trickling down my temples. I am breathing heavily, staring wildly at the darkness surrounding me. The boy I saw in the dream was me! 'Is that real? Will I really...?' I take a few deep breaths to get a grip over myself. 'It's just a dream. It's alright. I'm not blind... I won't be...'

Everyone fights with the enemy within. In my case though, I'm not sure if the enemy is blindness or my fear of this uncertainty. Here I am, fighting those feelings, barely able to prepare myself for the bigger battle. It's vital that I stay calm and confront whatever degree of impairment, or even blindness that might trouble me. But I am scared. Do I need help? Perhaps I do. Not just me, I feel my family too is chasing illusions of a condition in which it is impossible to find a cure. But when only a few people have the awareness or time, how will we ever get that help?

In the absence of a remedy, all I can do is remain patient and gather whatever strength I can muster, and see if I can confront the challenges.

TEN

The Persisting Blur

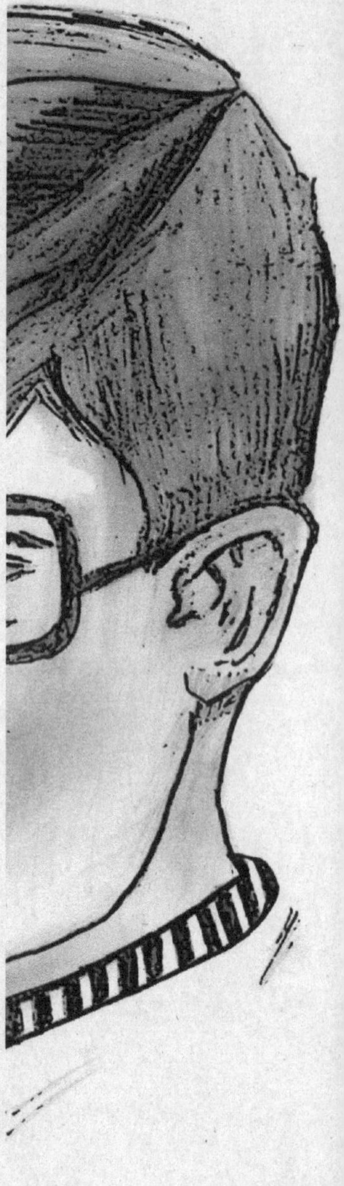

I've had worst days at school before, but nothing beats this one. It is irritating to stand straight for the duration of the class hour. Yes it hurts the knees a bit, but that's nothing compared to the humiliation of having to stand before a bunch of first years. If things had gone smoothly, my juniors would have looked at me with respect.

The class began alright. The teacher was writing a calculus problem on the blackboard and I was busy jotting down the steps in my notebook. My eyes trailed a few lines from the top of the board but suddenly my vision started to blur. Thinking that this is because of the sunlight ricocheting from the entrance, I try to write. Light covers almost half of the board. I blink and try to trace the white scribbling which should be clearly visible over the black surface despite the light. But I find it blurred. 'Oh! Will it be bad this time too?' I close my eyes and try to push away the thought. I then relax my eyes for some time and stop exerting it too much. I also try a technique that a therapist had taught me to relax the eyeballs. I slump on my desk and cover my eyes with cupped palms. 'Observe the darkness. Allow your eyes to remain still. This would make you see better,' the therapist had said, and nothing seems better than keeping the eyes in the dark for a while. But my exercise is interrupted by the teacher's voice.

'You! In the back row...stand up!' I stand up slowly, leaning against the desk.

'Have you copied the steps?'

'Yes...yes sir.'

'Then let me see it.'

He peered down at my notebook, lifted his head to look at me, and I saw his bloodshot eyes.

'I wrote this on the board some ten minutes ago. You haven't even copied the next two steps. If I'm not wrong, aren't you a detainee from last year? For how long do you want to warm these benches?'

'No, Sir, I had this irritation in my eyes. I was just resting them for a minute...'

'That's a nice way of saying that you've been sleeping.'

'No Sir, I...'

'You don't have to explain! Remain standing for the rest of the class and copy from the board.'

The urge to tell the truth was strong, but the teacher would have caught the slight hesitation in my expression and taken it for a lie to cover up my sluggishness. Yes, it's difficult to explain the blurring, especially when I'm not even sure if it's a symptom of my condition. So I thought it sensible to keep standing with a sorry face, rather than trying to explain something that's not even clear to me.

Thus, the blurring continues, paralysing my senses at the most unexpected moments. In a busy city where chaos is as common as street dogs, my disturbed vision makes me feel powerless, as if I'm an accident waiting to happen. And there are times I realize that I've come close to harming myself.

One day when I tried boarding a bus, it suddenly started to move. But the growing distance between me and the bus did not discourage my attempt to step on the footboard by sprinting towards it. The idea of giving up wouldn't occur so easily for someone used to such adventures. My vision blurred and I failed to notice the bus picking up speed and moving far away, until I was precariously close to colliding with a cyclist riding in the wrong direction.

The blurring is usually so sudden and so effective in unsettling my movement that I don't feel normal despite seeing normally for the rest of the time. At least an agile sprint to board the moving bus seems beyond my abilities, though I hate to think that I can't do that anymore. My condition is such that to me a mirage looks like a stream and a stream seems as faint as a mirage. The serpent and the rope scenario is not a philosophical contemplation, but a disconcerting reality of my vision. The bad news is that I don't know how to handle it; I don't know if it should be taken seriously or ignored. Of course, appearing paranoid before Dr Rakesh and hearing him say, 'It's not as bad as you think,' is more embarrassing than the classroom punishment. But as things stand, I don't have the luxury of sparing myself from that.

'The half-term results are out', a first year rookie cries out as he settles down on his seat in the classroom. The corridor outside is a beehive of activities with students rushing towards their classes before the second bell. We all sit in unusual silence, throwing anxious glances at the entrance, waiting for our teacher. As he walks in, we notice his pencil-thin fingers clenching a bunch of folded answer sheets. So...this is the moment.

In the afternoon, I hasten my steps back home, barely managing to control my excitement. I've done well in the exams and I can't wait to share the news with Ma. A good score in half-term exams may mean nothing in ordinary circumstances, but now any news is good news for us, especially when it is as rare as rain in summer. I exchange a quick high-five with Arjun and run towards the kitchen. Before words escape my mouth, I find Ma with a sheet of paper which, I observe, has the familiar scribbles of her brother, my uncle.

The news of my younger aunt's headache, which has got something to do with her eyes, is a big enough concern for Ma to dismiss my exam results with an absent nod.

The aunt in question is my grandma's niece who had been married to her own son. 'Consanguinity...' Dr Rakesh's words echo ominously in my mind. It is not as rampant as it once was during my grandfather's days, but it is still widespread to be a major concern. A few months ago, Ma wouldn't have thought a great deal about her cousins settling marriage between their kids, but now she would at least make a discrete attempt at caution. She can't talk directly because no one likes negative talk when a marriage is finalized.

The letter doesn't specify how serious the condition is, but the mudslinging between my father's and mother's side of the family, over who contributed the defective gene, still lingers in our minds. The latest news therefore is a cause for concern. My aunt's trouble could be pointed at as an evidence of the defect notwithstanding lack of scientific proof. Ma appears concerned.

'Why don't you go to her place and find out if she's alright? We can't change anything if her condition is terrible, but we can at least feel easy if things aren't as bad as we fear,' Ma tells me.

An agonizing groan escapes my throat. In the last few days, I've realized that operating in familiar environs and restricted space is the best way to get a grip on my recurring blur. Just when it's beginning to work, I get this request to visit our hometown. I love travelling alone, but I am also aware that doing it now will be like traversing through nine layers of hell.

Saying no, on the other hand, is equally difficult, given that Ma is worried.

We are seated in the patio of my uncle's house, watching the quiet street from the open door. A dog strolls by, sniffing at a pile of discarded fruit bags.

'Is it like...what happened to your grandma...the sudden headache and blindness?'

'It's not that bad. She had pain in her eyes, but her vision will be intact. Probably it's a little damage that can be made up with glasses. That's what the doctor said.'

The news that my aunt is fine brushes away my fears. In fact, I have felt so energetic after many days.

'I have a few letters to post. Why don't you take the bicycle and go to the Post Office? You always like to ride the bicycle, isn't it?'

The bicycle was the lure my uncle usually used to get me to run errands. It was something I had done without regrets during the two months of summer vacations I had spent at that small town. I take the bicycle keys and the bundle of letters from him. It's a bright afternoon, a day you'd not like to spend indoors. The ride is smooth until the end of the street, where I have to turn left and ride along the edge of the Bazaar Road to reach the post office. I'm just about to turn, when suddenly the blur comes back. This time it lasts longer than usual, sending jolts of pain through every inch of my body. I am drenched in sweat. My grip on the bicycle's handlebar slackens, and my body reels to the left.

On this road, there's none of the quiet and calm I had observed on the pathway outside my uncle's house. Buses connecting the town with the metro cities run along the road, along with sugarcane-laden trucks and heavy tractors. Pain weakens my body and I feel incapable of handling the traffic. I park the bicycle in a corner and wait for my nerves to settle down.

My uncle wants to take me to a pilgrimage. Is that the reference to blindness or my hesitation to saddle his bicycle that prompted him to include me for the forthcoming Sabarimala trip? I'm not sure. But uncle assures me he'd take me on one more pilgrimage with a large group, confidently predicting that I would witness a miracle. He's a guruswamy—pilgrim leader—in my hometown, and has been leading pilgrimages to the hill shrine for nearly 30 years. 'Oh I've seen enough of miracles and I'm not interested anymore,' I snap back, but I know how persistent uncle can be.

'How long can I stand here? I've to issue at least 40 more tickets. You better tell me where you want to go and give me the money,' the conductor's impatient voice jerks me out of my thoughts. I'm in the bus back home. The long journey and lack of rest is wearing me out and I feel more unsettled thinking of the blur that remained a persistent disturbance throughout this trip. In fact, I suspect I'm exhausted more by the stress of handling it than by anything else. My appointment with Dr Rakesh is just two months away and I'm determined more than ever to report the problem to him. Of course, I must ensure that I don't unduly end up spooking Ma and others. The urge to get home and hit the bed is overwhelming now as I massage my hands and legs and wait for the bus to take me back home.

Ma smiles at the news that her sister-in-law is doing fine, meaning we need not worry about any more triggers for a family feud on the issue. I deliver the information over dinner, badly wanting to hit the bed as soon as I can. The back-breaking, five-hour trip has been tiresome, accentuated by the eye disturbance. Ma kept suggesting rituals to some God or the other as an expression of our gratitude for saving aunt, but I hear none of it. Washing my hands, I crash on the bed and in a matter of seconds, drift off to sleep.

ELEVEN

A Timeless Vista

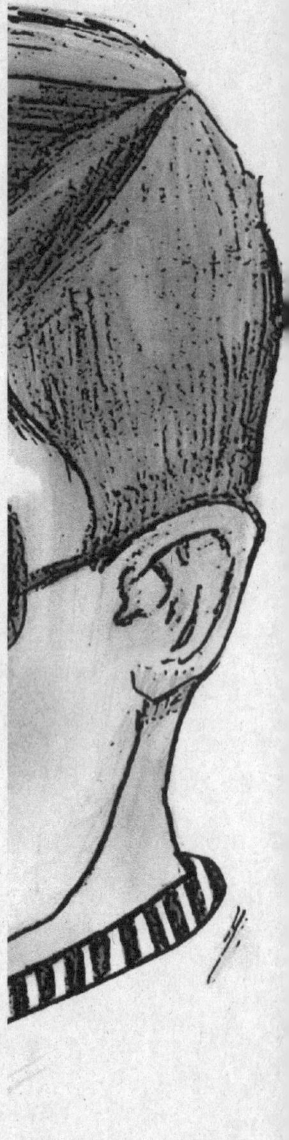

The plain white ceiling appears no different. I can say that because I've watched it several times in the last three years. Same as the man whose shadow covers the recliner I'm seated on. 'Keep steady. Don't shake your eyeballs,' Dr Rakesh instructs as he bends down to examine my eyes. For this test too the arrangement is as elaborate as before with the half-hour dilation and the arduous wait in the waiting area.

A sideways glance is enough to catch Ma's anxious face, notwithstanding the doctor's rebuke. We make eye contact now and then to reassure each other, and I feel it's crucial for Ma to stay easy today. I wouldn't like her to think this test as any different, especially when it's no different from getting the weather report: no matter how bad the news is, we can't quite stop the damage. But that's not how she looks at it. For Ma, the cure, the miracle that could save my eyes, exists somewhere and she wants to get it while my retinas are still healthy. She wants to know whether the medicines I'm gobbling down are actually improving my health or not.

'He looks better now,' Dr Rakesh says, observing me closely. A smile spreads across his lips, which is a good sign since we haven't seen that in our recent visits.

'You mean... his eyes are better?'

'They appear so. At least, I don't see a lot of dark spots spreading across his healthy retina. He should be okay now and I really hope the deterioration doesn't set in anytime soon.'

That's precisely the issue with degenerative conditions, as Dr Rakesh had explained during our previous appointment. There's no pattern to them. In some cases, the degeneration would be slow and insignificant and won't cause trouble for several years, but in other cases it's more of a freefall that throws the life of the patient off gear. The other problem, of course, is for doctors to remain cautious no matter how healthy the patient looks. When the existence of a condition like RP is confirmed, a doctor should be on his guard and make the patient feel overly optimistic. The reality is, even though your retinas are coping better for the time being, there's no guarantee that the situation wouldn't get worse in a few months.

'His retinas are fairly healthy now. He'll find it difficult to see in dim light conditions. That aside, he should be okay', Dr Rakesh says with a smile.

So, as Ma expected, my retinas are fine. None of us know, or even care, if my retina's stability is the result of the bitter pills and liquids or the more rigorous rituals performed on the cold granite floors of the temples. But the fact is, the immediate threat of blindness has dissipated and that's all that matters. And yes, I still experience the blur. But when the doctor says everything is fine, why should I feel scared about it?

No wonder then that it lifted the gloom and brought fresh excitement to our beleaguered home. Dad hunkered in prayers of thanks to Goddess Gayathri, while uncles and aunts joined in the euphoria. Incessant smiles have now replaced the usual, anxious frowns. Now, every day the radio is turned on for music. Ma's evening coffee is tasty again and I see her praying fervently before God, thanking the supreme force in the only way she knows. And I flip through my textbooks and notes without constant prodding to close them and rest my eyes.

While the threat of deteriorating vision still lurks,

we've had enough worries for a lifetime and are now looking ahead to times of revelry and merriment. Even lengthy prayers are nothing more than an expression of simple joy. After all, we need to thank God for this unexpected good news.

'May be this is the best time to take you on the Sabarimala pilgrimage,' uncle bellows on the crackling phone line from Virudhachalam, sounding as if he's calling us from some other planet.

'Let me think', I said not wanting to disappoint him by saying that I wanted time to prepare for my first year final exams. I was sure that this time I had a good chance of finishing among the top rankers.

I'm not sure what transpired between Ma and uncle, but one morning, as I was leaving for school, Ma declared firmly that I have to go on the Sabarimala pilgrimage to honour her prayers. This meant that I couldn't raise any objections or argue with her. I have to do whatever Ma says. Any hope of resisting a long and possibly boring tour at the expense of more urgent matters closer home, has gone.

It's hard to be a big fan of a group of pilgrims, especially when they are travelling with you on a cramped Matador van. The bus is also equipped with plastic stools to pack in additional passengers. I feel lucky to have got a window seat.

A simple trip to the shrine would have ended in three or four days, but uncle has scheduled a longer trip covering many temples across the southern states, which means we will be on the road for nearly 40 days. It's interesting to watch the landscape change from large swathes of brown earth to lush green fields and dense forests, as the van leaves Tamil Nadu and passes through Karnataka and Kerala.

Against my fears that the trip would be a tedious affair, spent largely in unending queues to the sanctum sanctorum, lengthy rituals, and boring drives, the journey across the three southern states is an unforgettable treat to my senses. Stepping into the cool waters of the tank at Talakaveri, I survey the peaks of the surrounding hills, the dense greenery covering its slopes, the glint of morning sun piercing through the dew on the tree leaves. The heaviness that seemed to weigh me down eased at the spectacular sight. With every inhalation of fresh air, filled with the scent of flowers and morning dew, I felt infinitely lighter and happier. The stress, the fear and helpless anguish simply faded away in nature's healing caress. My taut muscles relaxed as the cool water washed my limbs. Truly, the first dip in the water charged each cell of my body with energy and it seemed as if I had stepped over a live wire.

As I stood still, I once again observed the breathtaking vista around me, committing it to memory, wondering if I'd ever see anything so beautiful and uplifting.

The scenic beauty that trailed our path supplied me with more energy than my 16-year-old frame could hold. No, none of them was as invigorating as Talakaveri, but they kept me revitalized. At times I really wonder whether this 40-day experience had been programmed for a reason greater than merely getting rid of my mounting stress.

The sun was a mere splash of pinkish orange over the western horizon as our van clambered the Chamundi hills facing Mysore city. Long shadows of the trees left an intriguing pattern of dark patches on the road that ended at the Chamundi temple. We were in time for the evening prayers before the night that was to herald the new year of 1990. For some reason, uncle had made up his mind about halting in the hills for the night.

I reclined over the van's open window, observing two pilgrims, police constables, engrossed in an animated conversation. The men were discussing about a crime that had taken place in their town. The topic changed and my interest palled. Soon, one of them checked the watch and declared that it was time to retire. They left the seat next to me and the van fell silent. Since I wasn't feeling sleepy and was anticipating the New Year which was just hours away, I stared out of the window at the peaceful night lit up by the moon's soothing silvery rays. From the edge of the temple compound, where our van was resting, I could trace the hill's slope. As I peered down, I noticed the majestic Mysore palace down below, silhouetted in the sodium vapour lights that lined the road. Cars crawled over the blacktop with shining headlights and streets were lit with matchbox sized buildings. 'What's that?' I was lost in the beauty of the vista below. 'Did I enter some magical world by mistake? Or did I fortuitously step into the aboard of some God to earn his wrath?' My chest ached with the burden of breathlessness. As I released the air, I found myself in tears, partly in gratitude for the magical sight and partly for the mystery that life had become. Would I be seeing more of these mesmerizing images or was this some kind of a finale before the lights went out forever? I seemed to have drifted away thinking of the image that underlined the pleasures of sight and the terror of its slow decline.

Weeks after the trip, I kept thinking about the images of mountains and green slopes, stepping right into that vision and feeling cleansed as I did that morning. Of course, my mind still harks back to the magical vista of Mysore, but the conflicting feelings of mystery and misery keep pulling my heart.

TWELVE

The Descent Begins

September 1990.

It's the same path I've taken for several years now. Take a left turn from my street into Wall Tax Road, then walk straight past the fish market, the Post Office, and the Southern Railway building all to the left, cross the road and enter Madras Central. Pedestrians here have to share the road with the vehicles and stray animals as the footpaths are encroached by shops, parked vehicles, and a few homeless families. As I walk through the chaos, I rely on the familiarity—a kind of mental picture of my surroundings—to navigate instead of my eyes. No. I'm not blind, but I'm fighting the obscurity with greater frequency than before and find little respite. But mental pictures cannot be trusted for their accuracy, especially in a place as disorderly and chaotic as this one; and the possibility that I might collide either with a moving vehicle or a stationary one makes my step hesitant. My body shivers in the dreadful anticipation of colliding with the hard metal and chest heaves in terror.

Over the years, I've seen many watchful pedestrians and cyclists perish on this very road. A couple of them were run over by a speeding auto rickshaw before the Post Office, the very spot I cross now. 'Their brains were splattered all around,' said a neighbour who had witnessed the ghastly accident. And then there are also those not-so-serious collisions between pedestrians and cyclists that happen all the time here.

I hate to think of the way vehicles mow down people in these parts, but I cannot stop myself from repeatedly imagining being knocked down by a speeding cycle or bike. I'm not quite worried about injuries, but if the injuries were minimal and if the rider were to ask me the oft repeated question peppered with expletives, 'Don't you have eyes?' I can't think how mortified I would feel. I could take the abuse like most pedestrians, but in my case that question would be chillingly close to reality.

Of course, the haziness that troubled me last year had ceased for sometime after the good news from Dr Rakesh and the subsequent trip to Sabarimala.

The doctor almost repeated every word he had said before when we went back for a check-up two months back. Listening to him was like watching the weatherman showing different maps but essentially saying the same thing. 'His retinas continue to be healthy,' he declared, smiling like he always did. Everyone was happy, of course, so long as the therapies seemed helpful.

But the obscurity returned with a vengeance, freezing me in the middle of the chaos and dreadfully closer to moving vehicles. It seemed like a timely reminder to all of us that predicting the progression of RP is only as easy as forecasting the movements of a cyclonic storm. We in Madras know it better, having seen many a nasty storm change its course at the last minute to mess up some coastal town in Andhra or Orissa up north. Just when we felt that the therapies were turning out well, the blur, occurring with alarming frequency, reinforces the fear that I'm not quite out of it.

Just at the turn of the year, things appear to be under control. The second shot at the first year higher secondary was predictably successful, reinforcing my belief that I'm better prepared for the forthcoming public board examination with regular schooling. Throughout the first seven months, there was nothing alarming about my vision, except for the occasional lapses for which I was thoroughly prepared. It needed intense blinking or a second or two of resting the eyes to put aside the momentary lapse. My visit to Dr Rakesh confirmed that I had nothing serious to worry about.

But a week after the check up, I felt the haziness smudging the contours of the objects I was seeing. It wasn't exactly unusual but for two things: the blinking didn't help, and the obscurity lingered longer than usual. Just when I thought I had figured out how to handle the condition, it sprang in as a surprise. There were times when I was left in a busy street blinking furiously, gnashing my teeth in frustration, and squeezing my palms. Feeling helpless might seem alright, but I was feeling hopeless. Getting out of these nightmarish situations has been like trying to get up from the floor after being knocked down in a boxing ring. Funnily enough, one of the things I do—rather the only thing I can do—in these situations is, take a deep breath and count till hundred. While doing so, I try figuring out if my vision is back to normal or not. Even after things look okay, it's often impossible to walk normally. My steps, in fact, are uncertain and reluctant, and it seems as if I'm walking into something...something like a pile of broken glass pieces.

It is 8.45 am and I have got just ten minutes to catch the bus. The dreadful thought of standing before the headmaster's room and offering excuses prompts me to increase my pace a little, despite the lingering fear that a sudden and prolonged lapse might cause a nasty collision with a vehicle.

I go past two lanes without much trouble, but at the corner of the third lane just before the Post Office, which is a detour for many vehicles to dodge signals, my vision starts to blur. I should have figured it out earlier and stood at the corner, but it's too late for that. By the time I slow down my pace and start blinking, I am in the middle of the street. 'Get back... You'll get into trouble...' a terrified voice within my head yells like a danger signal. But before I can act on it, an auto rickshaw turns into the lane at blinding speed. I move backwards to avoid a direct collision, only to come in the way of two bicycles turning around the corner behind the auto. I freeze when I feel the rear-view mirror of the auto rickshaw brush against my shoulder and the front tyre of one of the cycles roll over my left foot. For a split second, the vision of splattered brains pops up in my mind. I don't want to die in an accident. Who will tell Ma? What will they tell her? The thought scares me.

I breathe heavily, and close my eyes as tears roll down my cheeks. I'm too feverish to realize that I haven't actually fallen down or met with an accident. Apparently the cyclist had applied brakes. He takes me to the corner of the road, where I lean over the billboard of a tea stall. I shudder violently but my eyes remain firmly shut.

I take out a water bottle from my bag, open its lid and drain it out in one huge gulp. The breathing slows down and my body starts to relax. I open my eyes slowly and find a crowd gathered around me.

'Are you alright?' someone asks as I look at the faces.

'Ye...yes,' I reply hastily. My heart is still pounding heavily and throat is dry despite drinking so much water. The crowd gradually disperses. I wait for a few more minutes to steady myself before stepping off the pavement and proceeding towards the bus stop. Spending twenty minutes outside the headmaster's room is as frustrating as I feared, but having escaped a fatal accident, I've nothing to complain about.

❧

Despite troubles in seeing during daylight, I can see clearly at night, thanks to the quirkiness of RP. There are enough rod cells—responsible for vision in darker environments—among the photo receptors, to allow me to see properly at night. I might stumble when I walk into a dark room from a brilliantly lit or sunny place, but once my vision is adjusted to dim light, I have no problems in seeing. In broad daylight, I often mistake a shadow for an object or stoop with squinted eyes while trudging through the uneven footpaths of Madras Central. So when I experience disturbance for the first time at night, it leaves me with a sinking feeling that my vision is probably going downhill. My first thought is that the deterioration has become rapid despite Dr Rakesh's assurance to the contrary, which, by the way, had been made with adequate qualifiers.

Unlike the previous lapses, the night time disturbance is accentuated by powerful flashes which are similar to the flash light going off in a camera. It's mild most of the times, but I'm thrown out of balance on days when it gets brighter and more frequent. Sometimes, the flashes are so distracting that it is difficult to guess how dark a place is.

I eventually learn from Dr Rakesh about the cause of such lapses. The photo receptor cells which sense light begin to decay for a person with RP, resulting in disturbances in vision. The electrical pulses that trigger the transmission of images to the brain, called photopsia, however, continue working despite the decay, causing flashes to occur.

Walking safely through the congested lanes around home has become a challenge for me now because of the recurrent flashes. I no longer feel confident or even enthusiastic about such walks. Waddling through the swamp of vehicles and pedestrians used to offer me anonymity before—the feeling of getting lost in the crowd. It also used to help me clear my mind of an argument at home or a fight with a classmate. These days, when Ma wants me to run an errand for her, I often feign exhaustion. At times I also complain about piling school work or the need for Arjun to assume more responsibilities.

In reality, the push-carts laden with heavy iron tools, rickety cycle-rickshaws, bullock-carts, and other unconventional vehicles, that run along Park Town's bustling streets, make me concerned about my safety.

'Are you making excuses because you don't want to step out of the house?' Ma asks me one day.

'Why do you think I'll do that Ma?' If I sounded indignant, it was more out of worry that she'd find out about the extent of my discomfort. After all, I'm supposed to report about any aberrations and troubles related to my eyesight, but I also wouldn't like to press the alarm bell for every little problem.

'Is it unusual to feel tired? I have had to run around a lot at school these days, and my legs hurt.'

Ma makes a sad face which confirms that I've hit the target; that at least she's buying my story for the time being. Emotional charades apart, my family knows that as far as my vision is concerned things have started to go downhill at some level; but we are afraid to voice it aloud. Probably, that's our way of wishing away the inevitable. To put Ma at ease about my troubles, I volunteer to meet the latest godman we have been referred to.

'Your fever is pretty severe, Ma. Besides finding

that place won't be so difficult,' I assure, requesting her to take rest that afternoon.

The godman shows me to the prayer hall, which has a montage of Goddesses adorning its walls. Goddess Maari Amman's image is prominently displayed in different postures: one is covered in neem leaves; another is clothed in a bright, yellow sari; and the most striking one has bulging eyes and a long red tongue hanging down her chin.

The godman's prayers include singing a few hymns and offering flowers and fruits. The prayer session is capped by him cutting a full lemon into two exact halves by placing it between his index and middle fingers.

But for the half moon casting pale light over a few scattered houses, the place is completely dark and eerie, especially when I watch it from the deserted bus stop where I stand and wait for the bus to Central. The last direct one, I learn, has left the place some time ago. It is 10.45 pm and I'm fairly certain that the bus service would have come to a stop by now. Standing virtually alone in a deserted place seems like a bad ending to a long and weary day. I could easily be mugged and left alone, or land myself in a ditch or an open manhole because of a sudden lapse. I didn't really want to be left stranded all alone for the next three or four hours. Ma must be worried, and it is already too late to call anyone now. I'm sure she must be cursing herself for agreeing to send me alone. My anxiety increases with each passing minute, accentuated by howling stray dogs and the deafening silence around.

After waiting for some time, a bus stops by. If I want to get back to home, I must first get out of the place. So I eagerly board the bus, without checking its final destination. It drops off the few last passengers at a place where I know a suburban railway station exists. It must be a 15-minute walk from the main road. Asking the way to the station from a fellow passenger, I enter a desolate street and hope that I'm heading towards the right place. At first, the flashes seem nothing more than a few shimmering bolts of light, much like the lightning before the summer showers. It slows down my steps, but it isn't perturbing enough to stop me. The continuous bolts combined with the strong smell of rotting vegetables coming from the trash on either side of the street churns my stomach with fear and repulsion. I realize that I'm crossing an empty vegetable market.

'What do you want?' asks a voice that slurs and struggles to put together the question. The sour odour of local liquor seems milder than the unpleasant smell around, but it is strong enough to warn me that I could be in danger. I decide to run back to the main road and locate the nearest police station. But I realize that I wouldn't be able to do either before being overpowered by the man. Facing the man, who is struggling to stand straight, I wonder how I landed up in this difficult situation. Nothing at the moment sounds as stupid or as naïve as the decision to visit the godman alone. 'God! What was I thinking?'

'Looks like I've come the wrong way. I want to go to the suburban station,' I say, trying to sound nonchalant.

'You...you...,' he stammers and I find it difficult to comprehend if his crooked finger, pointing at my direction, is a sign of trouble or the struggle of a heavily drunken man.

'You should have taken the road going towards right. N...ow, wa...lk ba...ck the sa...me way a...nd take the l...as...t left. You...will re...each the sta...

tion in ten minutes,' he slurs, spraying his arrack-laced spittle.

The Goddess seems to be working miracles for me I think as I trace back my steps to the main road. The 'road' suggested by the drunkard is nothing but a narrow, muddy trail that runs parallel to the railway tracks. I slow down and try deep breathing to clear away the regular flashlights. But I realize that the light around gets brighter by the minute. Just then, the ground rumbles mildly and an electric train's whistle pierces the silence. It must be the station I think to myself, and climb up some steps that seem unusual for a station.

Any relief I may have felt earlier turns into panic when an odour similar to that of the drunken man down the street assails me. Before I can do anything, someone grabs my wrist and pulls me into a crowded place, which, I notice now, is not a station.

'What's your brand, son?' a gruff and obviously drunk voice asks me. It takes me a minute to adjust to the bright light that surrounds me, and when I can see better, I notice a rack full of bottles and a counter where they are being exchanged for wads of dirty bills. A liquor shop! My heart thumps loudly, and I feel I'd faint if one of them were to touch me again.

I dash towards the entrance and don't wait for my eyes to adjust to the dim lights. I ignore the flash and run as quickly as I can. I notice a well-lit building towards my left. I am now sure that this is the Central. I find my way towards home without further ado.

All through the night, I toss and turn in the bed, trying to put away the frightening images of that evening. I must be incredibly lucky to walk back home alive. No, it wasn't the drunken men, but the panic that drove me from the liquor shop. It's still a mystery how I paced up without banging into any standing vehicle, person, or stray animal.

Now I'm pretty sure that the flashes are a part of my decaying visual perception and they are far more dangerous than complete blindness. Having lived with this horrible reality for a while, I'm used to the fear and panic that freezes me every time my vision is obscured by the smoky blur or the flashes. But along with fear and doubt, I also have one more feeling to grapple with: shame. Little did I know that these signs of RP could introduce me to a whole new feeling, the one I had virtually forgotten about after childhood, the time when I ran around with glasses. Nothing scares me more than being humiliated before my peers and classmates. I don't want anyone to go through such embarrassment irrespective of their physical condition. I feel I don't have a choice because I have an eye condition that is unlikely to give me a blissful death, or, at least, swifter blindness.

Even when my sight remains largely trouble free, I feel I am at a stage where I have to make a guess to recognize whatever I see. 'Is that the shadow of the plant, or is there a bike parked close by?' 'Is that a classmate who walked by? Or did I mistake that cleft chin?' Doubt follows me like a shadow wherever I go. I know that I'm not exactly fighting RP, but the fears, doubts, and every discomforting feeling that comes in its wake. Even on rare occasions, when I feel confident enough to walk, I dash against a wall or an open windowsill. At times, I have even been close to falling down the edge of an open corridor at school. Hurrying to the classes, I often find my friends and schoolmates pulling me away from banging into a wall or off the edge of a corridor. It's harder to even guess what those people think when they watch my faulty steps. All I can manage is blink frantically, trying to clear away the blur and walk along nonchalantly, as if nothing has happened.

'What's wrong with you? I've never seen anyone so arrogant before!' tells a classmate one day.

Arrogant? Well, I've been known as a nerd and ignoramus before, but arrogant, never. 'Why do you think I'm arrogant?' I ask the boy in utter bewilderment.

'What else do you call someone who refuses to shake hands with you or give you a high-five? You've been doing that to me for quite some time now.'

It occurs to me then that I can't see his face and the outstretched hand clearly. This is a sure sign that my vision is deteriorating even more rapidly than before. The misty smokiness that I see around objects is in fact growing thicker with every passing day. And now, I know that I can only see parts of an object and not the whole thing. I consider telling him the truth, but immediately dismiss the idea. Having heard him call me arrogant, I wouldn't like him to think that I'm a liar too. Who in the right mind would anyway believe that I can see clearly and yet cannot? It is because the smoky cloud obscures only the contours of my visual field. To save myself from further embarrassment, I try my best to stay back in the classroom during school hours, not even stepping out for my favourite afternoon stroll in the playground. My polite refusals to accompany friends are met with bewildered looks and nods that seem to confirm that I'm, indeed, arrogant.

One afternoon, I find my growling stomach too much to put up with and I decide to head towards the canteen. The place is packed with students in pink and brown, the colours of our school uniform. The boys fill the cluster of chairs to the left, while the counter to my right is busy as usual with boys either placing orders or collecting the dishes. I turn right, towards the counter, when I notice three boys moving to my side. Their hands seem to hold something and they are busy looking for empty seats. For a moment, it seems that I'm away from them, so I am not careful. When I'm just a few steps away from the counter, thinking about what to order, my hand hits something hot. It occurs to me that I've hit a cup of coffee in the hands of one of the boys, which is spilt all over, including his clean shirt. The boys stop talking and look at me in horror and indignation.

'What's wrong with you? You saw us walking this way and still came straight at us! Do you want to make unnecessary trouble?' the boy shouted. A simple sorry could have diffused the tension and saved me a lot of embarrassment, but nervousness chokes my throat. There could have been a yank of my shirt, a slap, or even a strong punch on my nose, but the boys withdraw quickly, showering me only with the most horrible of curses.

My battle with failing vision is now getting more and more difficult. The scars are deepening with every passing day. My standing posture has changed from upright to a defensive stoop. I now walk with bent knees and the dreadful anticipation of colliding with objects on my way. My swagger is reduced to hesitant steps to save myself from the embarrassment, and the rush of panic freezing my other senses seems like the most natural thing. I am seventeen and still have the best part of life ahead, but I feel old and defeated with each 'incident' chipping away my confidence. If this were to be my life, blindness seems like a blessing. If someone had told me that he'd welcome blindness and accept it more in relief, I would have laughed at him, but now, anything seems better than this hell.

Acknowledgements

This endeavour would not have been possible without my friends Ashwin Chand and K.C. Vijaya Kumar, who sparked my interest in books and writing from our early days when we were together in college. Thanks to Mark Malatesta of Literary Agent Undercover, Colorado, USA, for providing direction and focus.

My friends Venkatesh Ganesh and Tracy went through the initial draft and offered valuable feedback, while Anandhi Viswanathan spent hours critically evaluating the narrative and enriching it with her ideas. For my younger sister L.N. Gayathri, the months of writing this book was a special time to recollect various details of those harrowing times;

she was willing to travel backwards with me and reflect on all the memories, both good and bad.

My literary agent Kanishka Gupta of Writer's Side was not only excited about the story, but he assured me, with all his enthusiasm, that it would appeal to publishers and a wide audience. I hope he is thrilled as much as I am in seeing the book in black and white. Last but not the least my editor at Random House India, Milee Ashwarya and her colleagues. They proved the dictum 'to write is human but to edit is divine' a reality through their dedicated redrafting of the script.

My thanks would also go to *The Hindu*, *The New Indian Express*, *Times of India*, *Economic Times*, *The Week*, and other publications for their support in my early days. Mr Bashyam, Ms K.S. Latha, Mr L. Ravichandran, Mr R. Vijayaraghavan, Ms K. Jayalakshmi, Ms Janaki Murali, and several others sculpted my career at different stages.

I reserve a very special thanks to *Deccan Herald*, particularly to my current editor Mr K.N. Tilak Kumar and former editor Mr K.N. Shanth Kumar for giving me the chance to live my dream. Working for *Deccan Herald* for the past decade has been a wonderful experience, enriched by countless opportunities to write and work on new topics. All my colleagues have made me feel at home despite all my quirkiness. In their midst, I feel like being with my own family.

A Note on the Author

L. Subramani is a senior sub-editor and reporter with the *Asian Age*. He has been associated with a network of patients who are suffering from retinal diseases. This network helps reaching out to families and care givers in an effort to provide information, mentorship, and emotional support. He is also connected with the World Blind Union (WBU, Montreal), Retina International (Zurich), Foundation to Fight Blindness (FFB), the AMD (Age Related Macular Degeneration) Foundation, World Diabetes Foundation.

A Note on the Author

K. Srinivasan is [illegible] and [illegible] with [illegible]. He has been associated [illegible] who are suffering [illegible]. This [illegible] always [illegible]. He is associated with the World Wild Fund (WWF), [illegible] Foundation [illegible] Foundation.